WANTED

LAUREN BIEL

Library of Congress Cataloging-in-Publication Data

Wanted/Lauren Biel 1st ed.

Printed in the United States of America

Cover Design: Spellbinding Design

Content Editing: Sugar Free Editing

Interior Design: Sugar Free Editing

For more information on this book and the author, visit: www. LaurenBiel.com

Please visit LaurenBiel.com for a full list of content warnings.

I dedicate this book to all my usual readers who like what they like. I wrote this story entirely with you guys in mind. I hope you like Cole as much as I did (even though we probably shouldn't).

CHAPTER 1

It was a murder scene.

I was a murderer.

The moon sat high in the sky, illuminating the well-manicured lawn. I used the gold candle holder that sat on their fancy fucking dining room table to smash the window. Glass skittered across the floor as I tried to make it look like a robbery gone wrong. Which it was. I had used an unlocked door to gain entry, however, and I needed something a little more obvious. I cursed as the palm of my hand raked against a shard on the windowsill. Blood rose to the surface of my skin and as it dripped, it ran down my arm and blended with the blood on my t-shirt.

But the rest of the blood wasn't mine.

I ripped a piece of fabric from my shirt and wrapped it around my hand, tying it as best I could to stop the bleeding while walking toward the bedroom.

The woman was dead, lying in a pool of her own blood in the bed. The man? Beside the bed, face down on the ground. It wasn't meant to end this way. They were supposed to give up their money and cherished possessions.

They weren't supposed to fight. Shit, the man wasn't even supposed to be there. I watched the home until I thought I knew their schedule. I'm not sure how I got it so wrong. Could have been because of how incredibly fucked up I was.

It was neither here nor there, though, because it happened. I did what I had to do.

I rifled through their drawers and wallets, taking as much as I could carry. Money, jewelry, even credit cards. They wouldn't be able to report them missing. I memorized their birthdates from their licenses, knowing people like them probably used those special numbers for their pins, which was ill advised for this very reason.

I was a petty criminal—I usually ruined someone's day, not their life—but as I scratched at my arm, I remembered why I was there. Why I did what I did.

I needed more drugs. Meth, in particular. I'd been on a bad trip for nearly two days, caused by rank glass that made me angry and phobic. My mind was locked in a constant state of fear. *That's* why I went from petty to homicidal before I even knew what my hands were doing. Then it was too late. I was already stabbing them. First him, then the screaming wife.

I didn't look like your typical user, probably because I was still so new to being one. I looked at myself in the mirror as I scrubbed blood off my hands and tried not to get my makeshift bandage wet. The reflection staring back at me was familiar yet foreign. I still looked strong and muscled . . . albeit fraught with tension, which made my muscles flex. Drops of blood clung to my thick, dark hair. I put water in my hand and brushed it back, drawing the crimson away from my forehead. A drop of pink-tinged water dripped along my temple. Red, puffy skin encased my pale blue eyes, the telltale sign that I had been up for nearly two days without sleep.

I was too old for this shit. Who starts meth at thirty-five? Someone who went through a messy divorce. A man who lost everything he ever worked for. The drugs started as an escape and transformed into somewhere I wanted to live. I shook my head as I grabbed my baggy of white powder and poured some onto the marble countertop. I leaned over and snorted, inhaling the same garbage meth that sent me into a murderous delirium. What could go wrong?

I left, sneaking out the same door I came in. Sirens wailed in the distance the moment I stepped into the crisp night air. Darkness blanketed the earth around me. I tensed, my stomach clenching until I was certain I'd throw up on their lawn. I didn't know if they were coming to the scene of the crime, but the paranoia in my mind made me certain they were after me.

I took off across the lawn, racing into the woods. My legs slowed to a jog as I reached the tree line and a mere walk once I got beyond the trees. Branches broke beneath my feet as I walked. The darkness disoriented me. Tree trunks rose from the earth like pillars, and branches snaked across the gaps between them, as if trying to grab me. Every time my shirt hung up on one, I panicked, tearing more pieces off like Hansel leaving breadcrumbs back to the crime scene.

Fucking meth.

I kept going, alternating between panic and confusion, until I saw a modern A-frame house tucked within a clearing. Boxwood shrubs stood below the windows. Trees surrounded the home like a perimeter fence, and a pale glow shone from a single window. I looked back at the depths of the forest behind me. I wasn't sure how long I'd been walking. Being high on that stuff turned the concept of time into a complex math problem. I could have been walking for five minutes or five hours.

I focused my attention ahead of me once more and stared at the quaint home tucked away from it all. Away from the sirens. The murders.

It was the perfect place to hide out.

I idly scratched at my arm as I crept behind a shed and watched the home. There was no car in the gravel driveway. I hoped no one was home, but the glowing light in the window made me suspect someone waited within.

I reached into my pocket and pulled out the baggy of powder. I snorted another line off the snuffbox of my hand, inhaling deep, shaking my head at the burn slithering through my sinuses. As the amphetamine coursed through me, I tried to figure out my plan, A through Z. If no one was home, I might take a shower or a nap. I couldn't recall the last time I slept. But if it turned out there was someone there or if they came home, I'd have to kill them. I'd have no choice. The thought of murdering again made me ill. Or maybe it was the drugs. Both, probably. I teetered on the tightrope between mania and sanity. My thoughts raced over each other, merging into one lengthy vomit of syllables in my mind.

I snuck across the maintained lawn and shimmied along the siding of the house until I reached the front door. A single overhead light attracted waves of insects above it. I batted away bugs as I leaned over and tried the handle.

Locked.

I snuck around to a sliding glass door in the back of the house and peered through the darkness inside. Old, rustic furniture dotted the living room and attached dining room.

The stove clock read 5:55, which meant I'd been walking for hours, not minutes.

The screen door was locked. I grabbed my pocketknife, switched the blade, and sliced along the mesh fabric. With that gone, I reached inside and found the sliding glass door unlocked. People did that all the time—latched the screen door but not the door that kept people like *me* out of their homes.

Mud coated my sneakers, so I slipped them off at the back door. I stepped inside with slow and cautious steps. I was fighting the panic, trying to whip back my mania.

I kept my ears open for the sound of paws padding along the floor or the jingling of a collar that would alert me to the presence of a dog. I hated dealing with dogs. Nothing hindered the basic B&E like a damn canine. Thankfully, only the buzz from the old refrigerator reached my ears, and no food bowls or squeaky toys were anywhere in sight. I eased the sliding door closed, my jaw ticking as the paranoia ramped up.

I saw red and blue lights and ran to the window, pressing myself flat against the wall beside it. I leaned over, spread the curtain with a shaking hand, and relaxed with a sigh. They weren't really there. They couldn't be. I was in the middle of nowhere.

Fucking meth.

I closed my eyes and tried to will the delusions away. My heart raced against my chest wall as I pulled the baggy out of my pocket and realized just how little was left. Panic set in and rattled my muscles more than the accidental murders had. A whole-body fear that came from knowing I needed the drug—physically *needed* it—and had no way to replenish my stash.

Fuck me.

I was hearing things, which probably wasn't from the meth but from insomnia psychosis, which I guess was from the meth. My ex-wife's voice whispered between my ears with the condescending tone that made my blood boil. Her words danced in the air around me.

"You're worthless. You're never home. You can't even please your wife."

It shifted my high. The confidence—thinking I could get away with murder and live scot-free in this home—gave way to anger. I was pissed off. Maddened. I wanted to break things, like the globe light fixtures that dangled above the kitchen island, casting the glow I had seen through the window. Or the nice wooden rocking chair beside the fireplace in the living room. I imagined taking the fire poker and coming down on the arms of the chair or swinging it through the air and taking out the lights. I paced around the house, playing out violent scenes in my head and envisioning things I could break to leave a trail of destruction that felt more like the path of my life.

The sound of metal scraping against metal drew my attention to the front door. As manic as I was, I knew that was real. I stepped toward the front door, standing flush with the wall beside it. It opened inward, and a woman walked in. Her red hair bounced above her jacket as she hurried inside. When she closed the door, she saw me. I was struck by her for a moment, my tired blue eyes blown up in a stare that probably made me look crazy. I was beginning to feel like I was.

She screamed and ran for the stairs, dropping her purse on the hardwood floors. I shook off whatever froze me in place and chased after her. I caught her by the hood of her jacket and yanked her down the stairs. She screamed louder as she grabbed at my arms, kicking and flailing with unexpected strength.

But I was stronger.

"Shh," I whispered through clenched teeth as I let go of her hood and wrapped my arms around her to stop her from thrashing. I groaned as her full hips moved against my lap in her terror-fueled frenzy, the warmth of her pressed against me. Fuck. "For the love of all things holy, stop wiggling!" I yelled over her screams. If she didn't stop, I'd get too worked up to halt the thoughts racing to the front of my insomnia-driven delusion.

My mind wandered. I had a thing for big, curvy women. And redheads. There was something about wrapping my hand in those fiery locks of hair that made me ache.

I heard my ex-wife's voice again, echoing between my ears. *"You're a shitty husband."* I knew I was a bad person, but I wasn't half the shitbag back then as I was now. I had been a goddamn workhorse. And for what? So my wife could fuck the neighbor and run off with him? The thought alone filled me with white-hot rage.

"Please." The woman clutched against me squeezed out the word. I didn't realize how tight I had drawn her against me, cutting off her breath beneath her ribcage.

I tugged off her jacket and found her clad in a pair of purple scrubs. *A nurse?* I turned her to face me and locked on to her hazel eyes. Dark makeup encased them and streamed in thick lines down her cheeks. She looked terrified, but at least she'd stopped screaming, even though I could still hear it between my ears.

"What do you want?" she asked, her quivering voice choking off the end of each word.

I didn't know how to answer her. I wanted the opposite of everything my life embodied at that moment. I didn't want to be divorced. A drug addict. A murderer. On the lam and in her fucking house. But I could only think about how she'd feel.

I felt the devil whispering in my ear, his hot breath caressing my neck as he spoke. I heard his demands. I pulled her to the island, her flailing body fighting me with every step. My hand brushed the swell of her breasts before I removed her scrub top and threw it to the ground. Her scrub pants followed them, leaving her nearly bare and sobbing, pleading for me to stop as I pushed her chest to the granite countertop. She pleaded harder as I drew her panties down and worked off the buckle of my belt, begging for me to stop as I pulled myself out and forced my way inside her with hard and greedy thrusts that made the island rattle. She screamed out through sobs as I drew my hips back and ripped through her again and again. The more she begged, the harder my balls tightened, aching to fill her up.

What do you want? that voice asked again, but it was from somewhere far away. I shook my head and looked at her as she stood in front of me by the stairs, fully clothed. That sick but somewhat delicious fantasy was merely that. A fantasy.

Fucking. Meth.

"I need a place to stay," I told her.

"What . . . wait . . . why?" she stammered as I dragged her around the kitchen, still dodging her flailing limbs as I searched for tape. Or rope. Anything I could tie her up with.

"Where's the tape?" I asked, dodging her question.

"I'm not telling you," she whispered.

I stopped us both, holding her arm in a sure grasp. She winced as I tightened my grip and shook her. "Tell me where to find the goddamn tape, or I'll make my fantasy a fucking reality."

She looked at me with a cocked head, her forehead frowning with confusion, as if she was trying to understand what I meant. She didn't want to know what I meant. She just needed to know that I was manic, desperate, and fucking lonely. And I needed goddamn tape!

She motioned to a cabinet against the wall by the door, and I dragged her to it. I ripped open the door and found a roll of duct tape on a shelf beside her boots. I turned her around and pulled her arms behind her back. The sound of the tape ripping away from its spool echoed in the open room as I wrapped it around her wrists. I pulled out my pocketknife, and fear ripped through her at the sound of my blade, making her fight harder against me.

"Stop!" I yelled. I shook her arm and she stilled. I cut through the excess of the sticky silver, ripping it away from the roll. Only once her hands were secured behind her back did I let her go.

She sank against the wall with panicked, heaving breaths. "Take anything you want, just don't hurt me," she begged, flashing her desperate eyes at me. That look drew another fantasy from the darkest depths of my mind.

I pushed her down on her knees, keeping that soul-searching hazel gaze locked on me as she fell. Having her hands pinned behind her back accentuated her chest. She pleaded, begging me not to take her mouth, but it only made me work my pants off faster.

"Don't bite me," I snarled as I fisted her hair and forced her onto my dick. She pulled back, trying to get me out of her mouth, but she was exactly where I wanted her. I buried myself to the hilt inside her until I felt snot from her nose as she panicked and choked on my dick.

"I have money." Her voice broke through my fantasy.

I squeezed my eyes closed. When I wiped my hand down my face and opened them again, she was still standing there with her hands taped behind her back. Her eyes had dropped to my erection, which pressed painfully against my zipper. She panicked—*truly* panicked—writhing and straining against her restraints as she realized it wasn't money I wanted.

I walked away from her, taking enough steps to free myself from her scent. Like strawberries, sweat, and fear. I drew deep breaths into my lungs, reminding myself that I was a lot of things, but a rapist wasn't one of them. Well, I was also not a murderer until the devil on my shoulder told me to be one. And he was *screaming* for her.

"Drugs?" she asked, pulling me out of my mania. The devilish thoughts fell to a whisper.

Even though I was, in fact, on drugs, I took offense to her accusation. I walked over to her and fisted her hair in a rough grasp. "You don't know me," I said through clenched teeth.

"I know you're in a state of delirium," she whispered against the tension on her scalp. "Your pupils are blown. And you have nystagmus."

"What the fuck does that mean?"

"Your pupils are quivering. Vibrating. Meth? Are you on meth?" she asked.

Her analysis did nothing but piss me off. Fuck her. What did she know? Had she ever gone from having it all to living in a bedbug-infested motel? Did she know what it was like to hurt until drugs were the only escape from the hell burning around her? Doubtful. She was fucking beautiful, living in a nice house away from it all. I tugged at the ID on the pocket of her scrub top. She even had a great job. Vanessa Welch, RN.

"I can help you," she said.

"No one can help me," I said with a sneer. And it was true. Soon enough, I'd be hurting. Really fucking hurting. Once the drugs ran out, the devil on my shoulder would start to suffocate, and I'd crash like a motherfucker.

CHAPTER 2

S he continued pleading from her corner of the room. I had sat her down on the couch, propped her feet up, and turned on the TV for her. It was actually more for me so I could listen to the news as I tried to ignore the murmurs in my mind.

I thumbed through her purse, drawing out cards and cash. I pocketed her phone and looked at her driver's license. She was so young. I was over a decade older than her. How was I so fucked up and she was so . . . not. The roles should be reversed. It made me more bitter than it probably should have.

"Twenty-two? How does someone who's twenty-two have a place like this? And from Florida, at that." My words were short and filled with frustration and insecurity.

"It's my parents' summer home. They let me live here while I finished up my bachelor's in nursing at SUNY," she said as she adjusted herself to get the pressure off her wrists. "Can you please just let me go? You can take what you want and leave." She looked up at me with big, round eyes.

"Must be nice to have the support of mommy and daddy," I said with a sneer as I thumbed through her credit cards. I found a picture of her cozying up to a man. She looked so happy. Her eyes were squinting because her smile was so big. She was leaning on his shoulder as if she belonged there. If she thought it was love, it probably wasn't. Love was nothing but a fool's game. And I was the biggest fool of them all.

"Stop scratching," she said before dropping her gaze. Her words brought my movements to my attention. I was idly clawing my arm, cutting into my flesh without realizing it.

My eyes locked on her, and I wondered why she was being nice to me. She should have welcomed me scratching myself to death, not encouraged me to stop. I took a deep breath, full of longing for a deeper high. I went to scavenge in the bathroom, hoping and praying to the devil she'd have something lying around.

I picked up various bottles, reading them off and trying to find something I recognized. Something I could get high off of. She was as clean as a damn whistle. Nothing but over-the-counter pain pills.

I slammed the cabinet shut and met my own reflection. I looked like shit. Absolute shit. I rubbed my cheeks, grazing over my dark beard.

With a groan, I went back to the living room. "Do you have any—" My words were interrupted by the scene on the television. A banner danced across the screen.

Upstate New York. Double homicide. Suspect cut themself at the scene.

Vanessa remained silent, but her gaze shot to my hand, still bloodied and half-ass bandaged with the chunk of my shirt. As her eyes roved over my body, she paused on each spot of blood on my shirt and jeans. Everything came together in her mind. Just like that.

"You . . ." Her mouth gaped and the fear swept over her features once more. "You're wanted!"

Fuck me. I expected it to take longer for my grizzly crime to come to light. I was counting on the dark for a few days at least. Not hours. I think it had been hours. With the rising of the sun, things crawling in the shadows came to light, including my crime.

"Which means you should do everything I say," I snapped, "and once I can, I'll get out of your hair."

She made herself small as she backed into the corner of the couch, releasing sobs that made her whole body lurch. The sound whittled away at my last nerve. I had less than one fuck left to give her.

"For fuck's sake, stop crying!" I sat back and rubbed my forehead. The headache creeping over me signaled my need for more drugs. I reached into my pocket and touched the baggy. It comforted me, but I sure as shit couldn't get more once that was empty.

She stifled her tears, crying silently into the arm of the couch.

I got up and searched for her bedroom. It was the last room at the end of the hall, and a whoosh of strawberry-and-vanilla scented air assaulted me when I opened the door. My hand dragged along the dresser as I touched the perfume bottles resting on top of it. I lifted one, bringing it to my nose. It was half of the scent in the room. The other was a soft vanilla that clung to the first. My mouth watered with each breath.

I put down the bottles and rifled through the drawers. I

pocketed a small change purse with cash in it. A couple of prescription bottles stood on her nightstand—a muscle relaxer and something to take the edge off anxiety. I was ready to throw some of those back, but I'd need it once the withdrawal took hold. A sound came from the living room. I pocketed the bottle and hurried back down the hall.

I found her trying to reach the deadbolt with her hands still cuffed behind her. When she spotted me, she took off for the back door. I chased after her, but she got the handle open and made it into the yard. An earth-shattering scream that would wake up the whole goddamn world tore from her throat. I raced out and wrapped my hand around her mouth. She bit me, sinking her teeth into the spot on my hand where I'd snorted my drugs earlier. I clenched my teeth against the pain and ripped her back by her hair. She clamped down so hard that she tore my flesh as I snatched her away.

"Bitch," I snarled as the blood rose to the surface of my skin. I slapped her. Hit her hard enough to squelch her sounds and leave only the night noises. "I'm not trying to hurt you!" I dragged her into the house by her hair and slammed the sliding glass door so hard I thought the glass might crack.

Her wide eyes made her look like a whipped dog, and her reddened cheek puffed out where I'd struck her. She was an animal being dragged from the woods, its leg still stuck in the trap.

I pulled her into me, and my breaths rolled over hers. She inhaled sharply, trying to keep hers from crossing mine. My eyes hardened the more hers rounded with fear. Her chest rubbed against mine.

Fuck her, whispered the devil on my shoulder.

Just thinking about it made me swell with excitement. I

fucking wanted that. I wanted *her*. She was perfect, and if I'd met her anywhere else, I'd have asked her on a date. Instead, I was fantasizing about taking her against her will every which way I could.

She reeked of temptation.

"You won't be away from me for even a second now, little girl," I growled at her. "Come on, I gotta piss." I tugged her toward the bathroom and closed the door behind us, keeping a hand around her arm as I clumsily worked down my zipper. She tried to turn away, but I forced her to face me. She didn't have to watch, but I wanted to see her eyes.

When I finished, I washed my hand where her bite still marked my flesh, then dragged her toward the bedroom and pushed her into the center of the room. I flipped out my pocketknife and cut the tape off her wrists. She rolled her shoulders and touched the inflamed skin.

"W-why?" she stammered.

"Get undressed," I told her as I closed the bedroom door and leaned against it.

Heat tinted her cheeks and crawled toward her neck. "Pl-please . . ." she begged.

"Put something more comfortable on. I'm not going to touch you, if that's what you're worried about."

She chewed on the inside of her lip before she reached down and lifted the hem of her shirt over her head. Her arms instinctively guarded her chest. I tilted my head at the swells of her breasts beneath a sports bra. My dick hardened.

She went to the drawer and pulled out a loose t-shirt, shielding her chest with the fabric as she removed her bra. The devil on my shoulder told me to pounce, but I kept my feet planted on the soft gray carpet. A tear slipped past her cheek as she turned around to put her shirt on. My eyes roamed over the bare skin of her back. I twitched again.

"Can I leave my pants on?" she asked with shame coloring her cheeks.

I leaned over, opened a drawer, and tossed a pair of shorts to her. She looked away as she lowered her pants, the thin material hovering at her thighs as she tried to hide the hint of flesh between her legs. It wasn't just the devil who wanted to see that.

"I need a pair of panties," she whispered. Her eyes were on me as she backed toward the bedside table and pulled it open. She dug around in a drawer of brightly colored underwear, hesitating before she pivoted her body to reveal a goddamn gun in her hand. She raised it at me with her finger curled around the trigger.

The safety was on.

"That's a real stupid idea, little girl," I hissed.

She pulled the trigger, but she met resistance. Her face washed with fear as I stepped into her, and she tried to remove the safety. I grabbed the barrel just as she lifted it and pulled the trigger. A deafening gunshot exploded across every inch of the small room, and drywall crumbled above our heads.

I closed my eyes, my jaw ticking at the pain in my head, and gripped the metal harder. She recoiled from me as if I might hit her again.

"Rule number one of using a firearm for self-defense . . . know what condition your gun is in," I scolded her.

She whimpered as she collapsed to the ground, unwilling to release the grip. I shook it out of her hand and secured it down the back of my pants.

"I'm sorry," she whispered.

"Don't apologize for trying to defend yourself," I told her as I helped her off the floor. Her hands flew down to cover her black panties. "But I will put a bullet through your pretty head if you pull shit like that again. So thanks for this." I gestured toward her gun behind my back, and her shoulders deflated.

CHAPTER 3

I was hurting. My head throbbed, and my stomach felt like someone was spinning it around in an industrial strength washing machine. Day three of no sleep, and I felt the impending crash. I was basically there, hovering just in front of it. I looked at Vanessa's sleeping form on the couch. The need for sleep eventually surpassed her fear, but it eluded me. It had to. The situation was not ideal.

I tugged the baggy out of my pocket, poured some powder on the less fucked-up hand, and snorted. It hardly did a thing to quench the devil's thirst, but it would keep me awake.

When I sat up, she had just begun to stir. She woke up, swiveling her head as if trying to figure out if she had awakened from a bad dream. If she had, she'd gone from a bad dream to a living nightmare. The furrow of her brows, the panic setting into her breaths, and the overall look of disappointment in her expression made me feel a bit bad. There was a hint of disgust on her face, her lips drawn tight at the sight of me, which was fair. I looked like a psychotic, homicidal drug addict at that moment. I knew that.

"Can I please have water?" Vanessa asked.

The thought of it churned my stomach, but I got up and searched her cabinets for a glass. After filling it, I brought it to her. She stared at me as I offered it to her, forgetting that I had taped her wrists behind her back once more. It was hard to remember shit when your head was in a vise.

She sat up taller as I put the rim of the glass between her full lips and tilted it so she could drink. Water slipped past the corners of her mouth, wetting the front of her white t-shirt. I didn't try to pretend I wasn't staring at her nipples as they tented the fabric. When she noticed, her cheeks flushed and she stopped drinking.

"Thanks." She eyed me for a moment. "You don't look well," she whispered. Which was real fucking rude, but if I looked anything like I felt, then she was correct. "Have you tended to that cut on your hand?"

I looked down at the soiled black fabric wrapped around my hand. No, I hadn't thought much of it, except for trying not to get it wet. I loosened the tie and it spread away from my skin. The cut was deeper than I thought, with frayed edges that curled outward. I don't know how I didn't feel it, so wide open like that.

"Let me see it," she said as she leaned forward and craned her neck toward me. "Yeah, that's not going to heal on its own. You need a hospital."

"You're a nurse."

"Yeah . . . a nurse. Not a doctor."

"I'm not going to the hospital," I told her firmly. I was not about to walk into any medical facility with a hand injury when the news was still reporting about the murderer with an injured hand.

She scoffed. "I have some Steri-Strips, but you need something better."

I reached into my pocket and pulled out my knife, cutting through the tape again. She rubbed her wrists before taking my hand in hers. Her skin was cold, as if she wasn't getting enough circulation with her hands cuffed behind her.

"May I?" she asked as she stood and motioned toward the bathroom. Her voice had an edge of annoyance as she asked for permission.

I nodded. "I'll come with you."

I followed her to the bathroom, and she dug around for a box of Steri-Strips. She grabbed a bottle of alcohol and tugged my hand over the sink. She became methodical, as if she was working. Her touch was tender as much as it was firm, and I couldn't help but think she was probably an excellent nurse.

It fucking burned like the devil's asshole when she poured the alcohol over my wound. I puffed out my cheeks and tried not to scream out. My jaw ached from the pressure as I tensed it.

"Man up, killer," she said with a sneer, and it made my lips twitch upward. I wouldn't let them go all the way into a smile, though, and neither would she as she poured more of that hellish liquid into my cut. "What's your name, anyway?" she asked.

"I'm not at liberty to discuss that information," I said through clenched teeth.

"Fair enough."

When she finished torturing me, she blew on the cut, her cold breath soothing the residual pain. She applied the Steri-Strips and released my hand back to me. "That will do for now," she said as she wiped her hands on her shorts.

"But like I said, you need a doctor." Her eyes met mine. "And I need to go to work, you know."

"Call in."

"I can't just 'call in.'"

"You sure as hell can, Vanessa, and you will. Tell them you're sick. You'll be out the rest of the week. I'll be out of your hair by then."

"The week? You're going to stay here for a fucking week?" she asked with her mouth gaping.

"What'd you expect?"

"That you'd take what you need and get going."

I should have. That would have been the wise choice. But I was about to crash—hard—and what better place than with a nurse?

"And miss out on this world class TLC? No thank you," I goaded. Her lips tightened in anger. I felt like myself for a single moment. Well, the me I used to be.

"What else do you need? Your hand will heal."

I hardened my stare. "Withdrawal."

She shook her head. "I'm *not* helping you through withdrawal. *Way* beyond my scope. You need a hospital." She pushed past me and I followed her, half expecting her to go for the door again, but she knew her pistol rested at the small of my back and that I actually knew how to use it.

She spun on her heels to face me once more. "How many days have you been awake? You keep talking to yourself. Pacing around the house."

"None of your business," I snapped. Fuck her and her judgement.

"If you want me to help you, I need to know."

"Three days."

"And you're still on methamphetamines?"

"Don't be so clinical about it," I said with a groan.

"When was the last time you used?" Her nurse voice came out again—caring, with a hint of condescension.

"A little this morning. I don't have much left."

"When you crash, you're going to crash hard, and I don't have the ability to take care of you like a hospital would." Her gaze softened. I was tugging at her nurse heartstrings. I felt the pull between us. "I have some Xan —" she began, but I interrupted her by pulling the bottle from my pocket. "Thief," she snapped as she ripped it away from me. "Why the hell am I helping you?"

"Because you took an oath," I said with a smirk that dropped from my face as the nausea crashed over me again. I ran off to the bathroom and puked my guts into the toilet. No amount of vomiting cured the wringing of my insides, though.

I expected her to take the opportunity to run. I'd pocketed her keys, but she didn't know that. I thought I'd have to chase her down, and my body was not prepared for it.

She showed up in the doorway.

"How long have you been using? Daily?"

"This is beginning to feel like an intake form," I said, a gag chasing my words.

Her hand landed on her hip. "Are you going to answer or not?"

"Casual until last month. Then all day, every day."

"Do you snort it? Inject it? Smoke it?"

"I just snorted. I tried smoking it once . . . not for me. There's something uncouth about a meth pipe."

Her lips twitched, and I thought I might get a smile out of her, but she sobered real quick. "Any cardiac history? Ever had seizures?"

"No and no."

I rose to my feet and stumbled against the sink. My body demanded sleep, but my brain was still wide the fuck awake. Amphetamines crawled along the recesses of my mind, prodding me to keep my eyes open. And the devil still murmured in my ear. Had I listened to him and taken her like I fantasized about, she wouldn't have been willing to help me. Not a chance. But then again, she might have been waiting for me to crash into a deep sleep so she could escape. I knew I had to stay awake because I didn't trust her not to turn on me. I'd sure as fuck turn on me.

CHAPTER 4

It was nearing the end of day three, and somehow my mind still fought sleep. I found myself going manic again. Pacing. Talking to myself. Having conversations with my ex-wife. And Vanessa just stared at me, taking it all in. I didn't cuff her wrists behind her back again, but I taped them in front of her to make her more comfortable, at least.

The sound of the ticking clock on the wall assaulted my ear drums and rattled around in my brain. I was getting short and snappy, anger brewing beneath the surface as my body begged for drugs.

"I need to go to the bathroom," she whispered.

Sweat beaded on my forehead, leaving a thick sheen along my skin. I tapped my heel on the ground and bounced my knee up and down as anxiety ripped through me. "Come on," I snapped at her, harsher than I intended.

"I'm not going with—"

"Then piss yourself. I don't care."

She stared at me, blinking heavily. When she finally got off the couch, I followed her to the bathroom, leaned against the door, and glanced away from her.

"Do you have to stand there? I can't go with you here."

"Yes, I do." I folded my arms over my chest and kept my gaze averted. Out of the corner of my eye, I watched her huff and struggle to tug down her shorts. She caught the pockets and wiggled them past her thighs, and gravity did the rest.

While I waited for her to finish, I stepped into the hall, grabbed my baggy, poured a little powder onto the back of my hand, and snorted. When I walked back into the bathroom, she was struggling to get her shorts up from her ankles.

I cast my eyes on her as I stepped closer. "Do you need help?"

She had such sadness on her face as she nodded. She stood upright, her cheeks red from embarrassment, and I kneeled to grab her shorts and panties from the ground. I half expected her to knee me in the face, but she just stood there, eyes welling with tears as I was a breath away from her pussy. Even with the drugs leaving my system—and the devil clawing for air inside me—I thought about her. How she'd feel. The horrible imaginings pried into my mind once more.

I lifted her, putting her ass on the sink. She pushed at me with bound fists, and her pleas fell on deaf ears. In fact, it pulled more blood to my dick. I was so fucking hard as I spread her incredible, thick thighs, exposing the sweet flesh between her legs. Her face reddened as she cried. Her fists balled and pressed into my sternum when I pushed inside her. So goddamn wet. Heating my cock within her, I wanted to come inside her. Claim her like I claimed her home.

I blinked heavily. I was still on one knee in front of her. She was nowhere near the sink, and I was not balls deep inside her. At what point was it not the drugs encouraging such horrible thoughts?

I let out a deflated breath and pulled up her shorts and panties. I helped her wash her hands in the sink, but she wouldn't look at me. As if I had seen too much of her. Which I had.

When I caught my reflection in the mirror, white powder coated my nostril. I wiped it away and licked it off my finger. I couldn't let a single bit go to waste. My skull throbbed. I couldn't possibly do enough to head off the crash much longer. I had just enough to keep me a step ahead of it, but it was almost gone.

I guided her back to the couch, and she sat down with a huff. I lay back in the recliner and rubbed the bridge of my nose, trying to comfort the headache eating away at me between my eyes. Sweat dripped down my temples and landed on the fabric of the chair beneath my head.

My body was heavy. I was so damn tired. I hid her phone and keys earlier—somewhere she'd never find them —because I knew my crash was imminent. I also had to hide the gun and knives and anything else she could use as a weapon. But I had no idea what to do with *her*.

Once I fell asleep, I couldn't control what she did.

I CLEARED my sinuses with a deep inhale. The empty baggy burned through my pocket. I raced around the house, barring the doors with chairs and loose furniture. I kept looking out the window, seeing imaginary lights. Hearing sirens that didn't exist.

"You were such a bad husband, Cole. I've been fucking the neighbor."

"Shut your whore mouth!" I screamed, stopping in the middle of the room. My heart raced, thumping against the wall of my chest. I was delirious. It was my fourth day without sleep. I was riding the line of just high enough to stay alive but not enough to feel good. Amphetamines coupled with insomnia. Not good. Not good at all. It didn't help that the meth was garbage. Some batches made you feel the itch beneath your skin, while stuff like this made you feel like you couldn't live within your skin at all. Like hot ash beneath the fibers of your flesh.

The anxiety was surreal. I had paced the length of the house for the last several hours. I started taking cups out of the cabinets and stacking them on the counters. Plates were next. Those belonged on the floor, so I stacked them in neat towers at my feet.

I was losing my damn mind.

I felt a hand on my shoulder, and I recoiled from the touch with a panicked jerk.

"You okay?"

I heard the angelic voice, but I couldn't respond. I just kept stacking things in neat piles. A hand grabbed my arm, and I jerked my elbow back and made contact with flesh. A scream came from behind me. I dropped a glass and it shattered, bringing me back into the moment.

I turned around, wide-eyed and crazed, and saw that I had elbowed Vanessa in the face. A thick line of blood dripped from one nostril, and tears welled in her eyes. I searched for my knife, but I'd hidden that too, in case I fell asleep. I grabbed her wrists and lifted them toward my mouth. I bit into the tape, sawing at it until I could rip it apart, piece by piece.

"I'm so sorry," I told her as I wrapped her in my arms and pinched her nose.

She pushed at my chest, trying to get out of my grasp. Curse words flew out of her mouth as she swatted away my hands and clutched her own nose. She rubbed along the bridge, trying to assess if I'd broken it. "Fuck you," she snarled, blood staining her mouth. "You've rearranged my entire house. You're paranoid. You're out of control. And I'm going to take a fucking shower." She gestured to her face and hand—now covered in blood—and to her red-stained shirt.

She stormed off, leaving me too shocked to chase after her. I had sobered up enough to feel guilty as fuck about striking her. But I was unsober enough to realize I couldn't control what just happened, even if I wanted to.

The shower began to run. Pipes rattled within the wall. I turned to go after her, but the moment I pivoted my body, I had to turn back to vomit into the sink. Pure bile. Acid that burned my throat. I needed to force myself to eat something, anything. A sleeve of crackers on the counter sufficed, though I nibbled at them because eating was such a goddamn chore. I forced down what I could, but the salt on the crackers did nothing to cover the acrid taste in my mouth. I needed mouthwash.

When I cracked the bathroom door, steam billowed toward me. I snuck inside and closed the door behind me, slow and quiet. The moment I wrapped my hand around the neck of the bottle, my eyes darted to the shower. I saw her form through the frosted glass. Wide hips. Soft curves. Thick thighs that touched, leaving everything between them to the imagination.

I stripped off my clothes and climbed in behind her. She threw curses at me as she backed into the wall. I dropped to my knees in front of her, the water raining down on me as I spread her pussy and put my tongue against her. She flailed and squirmed, striking at my head with closed fists, but I gripped her hips in a rough grasp and kept my mouth on her. With my face buried between her thighs, I ate her like she was the only meal that would satisfy me. Her fists striking my head and shoulders became taps as it started to feel too good for her to fight me. She could hate me again afterward, but I just wanted her to come against my mouth.

A crackling sound brought me back into the moment. I was squeezing the neck of the bottle so hard I had bent the plastic. I'd liked to have lived in that fantasy for a little longer. I wanted to feel the upward curl of her pelvis so I could devour her better. I wanted to feel her spasm as she came. My cock ached. I knew she'd never allow it. She looked at me with too much hatred.

I grabbed the mouthwash and left, carefully closing the door behind me. I rinsed my mouth and spit in the kitchen sink, and the water washed it down the drain.

She came out in a clean t-shirt and leggings, her dark red hair in a bun on top of her head. Water dripped down her cheeks, and she wiped it away with a brash rub of the back of her hand. She still looked angry. Maybe more so.

"Why were you in the bathroom when I was showering?" she asked. Her words were laced with accusations I deserved.

I shook the bottle beside the sink. "I threw up again. I needed mouthwash."

"You couldn't wait?"

I could have. Most definitely. But tell that to my impulsive self when I was wedged between feeling amped up and sick as fuck. I could only focus on ridding my mouth of the vile taste on my tongue. "I'm sorry."

"The way you look at me . . ." she said. "It's fucking creepy."

"I haven't touched you," I snapped back, ignoring the fact that I'd had my dick inside her, her mouth on me, and my mouth on her in my head so many goddamn times. I'd gotten hard around her while my eyes roved over her curves. Sue me. She was beautiful. I wouldn't apologize for finding her attractive.

"Yet," she said with a scoff.

"Excuse me?" I stepped toward her.

"You're going to find yourself with little control very soon. Even less than you have now."

Fuck me. She was right about that. Pretty soon I'd suck the devil's dick for a hit of ice. The frustration and anger would become unbearable as my body fought my mind. But also, fuck her for thinking I'd force her now.

I stepped into her and tugged her up by the back of her neck. Her mouth was so close to mine, her jaw set in anger. "If I was going to force you, I would have by now. I would have when I had you squirming against my body or while I could smell your scent in front of my face. When I was on my knees in front of you, you were bare and vulnerable," I growled.

Red crept across her chest and rose to her cheeks. I didn't know if she'd smack me for what I said, but I was irritable and didn't need her shit when I felt the way I did. I didn't need her insinuation when I'd fought every urge to rip through her.

CHAPTER 5

S weat coated my skin with a sheen that chilled me. I trembled, my rattling teeth distracting us as we watched the television. I had crossed into withdrawal, into a freezing hell where every fiber in my body begged for drugs.

I shivered, unsure if it was from the cold or guilt as they showed pictures of my victims across the screen. They looked like good people—better people than I was—yet I'd extinguished their lives over what was destroying mine.

I guess we all died a little that night.

I glanced at Vanessa. Her eyes were glued to the screen. The television showed a clip of the body bags being carried out before flashing to images of the bloody scene. Her chest rose and fell rapidly, as if the panic was brewing, ready to boil over. If she panicked, I wouldn't have the energy to calm her the hell down. I didn't have the patience right then, and I worried I'd end up accidentally killing her as my body rippled with rage.

The banner blipping across the screen said that it'd been forty-eight hours and they still had no solid leads. Which was excellent . . . for me. Thank fuck I'd never gotten into trouble before. No DNA for them to link back to me. Not yet, at least.

"Why'd you do it?" she asked, her lips drawn tight.

"I didn't mean to. It was a normal robbery until it wasn't."

"Normal people don't accidentally kill other people."

I brushed my hair back, wet with sweat. "I wasn't normal. Wasn't myself."

I knew it wasn't me. Not who I really was. I never hurt a soul before my wife demolished my heart and took everything from me. But the drugs took over my life. I stayed up for days on end, becoming more manic by the hour. While chasing my next hit, I did things I wasn't proud of. Whoever *that* was, whoever did that to those two people, wasn't me. The real me felt like it was trying to burst through a diseased and dying vessel.

"You're a monster," she whispered as her gaze fell from the TV.

"I did monstrous things, but *I'm* not a monster."

She scoffed. "Keep telling yourself that."

God, I wasn't in the mood for the conversation that hung in the air between us. I fucked up. I messed up colossally. I'd never forgive myself for what I'd done. But I didn't need her to look at me with the hatred I already had for myself.

I was tense and exhausted. My body was so tired. My brain darted between awake and starved for the high it craved. I released a deflated breath. "I wouldn't hurt you," I whispered.

I didn't think she heard me as she got up and walked into the kitchen. She came back in with a pill and a glass of water, handing them to me without looking me in the eye.

"Here," she said with a tilt of her chin. "You need to sleep."

Fuck. I knew I did. But sleeping meant letting my guard down around her. It meant trusting she wouldn't kill me or run for the police the moment I closed my eyes. The way she looked at me—or couldn't look at me, rather—made it impossible to allow myself to rest.

At some point, my body would give out and I would sleep whether I felt safe or not.

I pushed her hand away.

I needed to figure it out before I let myself be vulnerable.

I PUSHED my back against the wall, my chest heaving with panic. I leaned over and drew the stiff curtains aside. It was dark outside, and the police lights flashed against the night sky. They screamed for me to come out. To give up. I covered my ears with my hands, trying to drown out the sounds.

My palm ached, my panic amplifying the pain. I felt *everything*. Too much. At that moment, I almost welcomed my death at the hands of the law.

The police said someone saw a bearded man leaving the scene. I heard them. When I opened the door, they stood along the tree line. They didn't have uniforms. They had on long jackets that even covered their feet. Their faces were blurred, but I somehow recognized every one of them. They looked like people I knew. My brother-in-law stood at the front of the line. I shook my head as he threw his hand up, and they marched toward the house.

I slammed the door shut and pressed my back against it. My eyes raced around the house. I saw her, Vanessa, sitting on the couch with wide eyes full of fear. She made herself small once more, pressing herself against the arm of the couch. My footsteps sounded like thunder in my ears as I walked toward her. When I grabbed her arm and yanked her off the couch, she flinched.

"There's police out there," I said.

"No there aren't!" she yelled back. "You're hallucinating from lack of sleep!"

I narrowed my eyes at her. I didn't trust her or anything she said. I *saw* them. I *heard* them. And they knew what I looked like. That I had a beard! Racing thoughts bounced off the walls of my mind.

I tugged her toward the bathroom, and she dug her heels in. When she did, I forced her steps with a rough grasp. I closed the toilet lid, sat on it, and lifted my chin toward her.

"You need to get rid of this," I told her. I rubbed a hand through the thick, dark hair on my face.

"Wh-what? I'm not shaving you!"

My lip curled. I stood and pushed her against the sink, and she fell backward, knocking the soap dispenser onto the floor. Her eyes were wide and fearful. My crotch pressed against hers, the heat of my erection against her lower belly. She swallowed hard, and I watched her throat as she did.

I reached behind her and grabbed the razor off the sink. I thrust it toward her, and she recoiled as if I was going to hit her.

"Shave my face, little girl."

Her teeth clenched. "I've never done that before."

"Today's a good day to learn," I growled as I wrapped her hand around the handle.

I sat down again and lifted my chin. Her hands shook as she turned on the tap, let the water run warm, and dipped the razor beneath the stream.

I closed my eyes as she started to glide the blade along my skin. She was so rough. "Slow the hell down," I told her as I grabbed her hand with mine and slowly guided her along my chin.

"Why don't you do this yourself?" she asked, a tremble in her voice.

"Because my hand is jacked up. And I want *you* to do it."

Her cheeks flushed pink with anger as she leaned back and let the water wash the dark hairs from the razor's edges. She placed it against my face again and kept shaving, though her hands wouldn't stop quivering as she tried to steady one with the other. When she rolled the razor beneath my chin, she caught my skin, nicking me. I reached up and touched the blood that rose to the surface and trailed down my throat.

"Fucking A," I said as I ripped the razor from her grasp, causing a fear-laced whimper to leave her parted lips.

Fuck, it was maddening. Her fear. Her fuck up. Fucking up because of her damn fear. I wanted to spill blood from her. Wanted to rip through her and watch her blood travel the length of my dick. Eye for an eye. I wanted to muffle her screams as I painted her pussy with her own crimson.

I looked in the mirror, trying to ignore my bloodshot eyes as I assessed the cut. I left her cowering in the corner as I finished shaving.

"Please . . ." She begged. "You need to sleep."

"You don't fucking know what I need!"

I needed drugs. I needed to stop feeling like I was bursting out of my own flesh. I knew I needed sleep. My brain was firing in all directions.

Angry. Paranoid. Horny.

It was like the devil was playing a game inside my head. Spinning a dial.

Vanessa reached into her pocket and pulled out the pill from before.

I clamped my hand over her wrist in a rough grasp. "How do I even know what you're giving me?" The devil's dial landed on paranoia, and I felt like she was against me too. She was *trying* to put me to sleep.

"Go take one from the bottle, then," she whispered, and her gaze dropped from me.

I went to the kitchen, grabbed the orange bottle off the counter, and read the label. I opened it, put three in my hand, and threw them into my mouth. The glass of water from earlier remained beside the bottle. Stagnant. I went to drink it but stopped the moment it touched my lips. She could have poisoned this water. I threw the glass in the sink, shattering it against the steel walls, and drank from the faucet instead.

I didn't trust anyone or anything. But I especially didn't trust the woman in that bathroom.

CHAPTER 6

I woke up with a headache so persistent I had to rush to vomit up everything I hadn't eaten. I heaved into the toilet. Fuck.

I looked around the bathroom. I wasn't yet in jail, so that was a good sign. I was alive, so that was another. I swished mouthwash, spit it into the sink, and watched the green liquid swirl around the drain as I ran the faucet.

Sleep was disorienting as hell, but my body wanted more of it. Unfortunately, the withdrawal symptoms wouldn't allow for such peace. I stood upright and looked at myself in the mirror. My chin was smooth.

When the hell did I shave?

Glimpses of memories filtered to the front of my mind. I remembered her shaving me. Her. Vanessa.

"Hello?" I called out.

There was no response. I ran to the bedroom, moved the metal register aside, and grabbed the gun and my knife. I left her phone and keys, again covering the dark cavern with the register. I raced into the living room, expecting her to have left. To have run off to find help. To get me put away where I belonged.

I found her curled up on the couch, drawn into herself as she slept. I looked at her right arm. It was bruised as shit. Bruises that mirrored the print of my hand. Fuck. *What'd I do to her?*

"Hey . . ." I whispered as I reached for her.

She leapt out of her skin, recoiling from my touch. "Fuck," she groaned as she wiped the sleep from her eyes. "You're awake."

"How long was I asleep?"

She looked at the clock on the wall. "Like . . . twelve hours."

I felt like I needed more. Twelve hours of sleep to counter the ninety-six hours and some change of being awake didn't seem like enough. My body felt heavy. My mind felt dead. As if it needed drugs to live.

I grazed her arm where the purple-and-pink bruise contrasted with her skin. "What'd I do?"

She narrowed her eyes at me. "You were in full-blown hysterics. I told you that you needed to sleep. Instead, you sat up, freaked out about the police, and made me shave your damn beard off."

"Did I hit you?"

She fumbled over her words, as if she was confused by my concern. "N-no . . . you just got really pushy."

"I'm sorry," I told her. I was sorry. I had no intention of hurting her. Memories flooded me. Several scenes of wanting to be selfish with her body. A shiver wrangled my spine. As much as I would take her in half a heartbeat, with a sobering mind, I had no interest in forcing her. Actually, my sobering mind made me feel really guilty for even being there at all.

Memories of the murders hit me across the face. I didn't remember the moments before the murders, but I remembered the immediate aftermath.

The blood.

The silence.

My lack of panic.

My finger rode along my palm, reminding me of the blood I left at the scene of the crime.

I had no choice but to be in this house. I commandeered this home for my own safety, and she was just collateral damage. I rubbed my chin. I hadn't had a smooth face since before the divorce.

"Now that you aren't tweaking, care to tell me your name?" she asked.

I didn't withhold my name because I was tweaking. I withheld that information because I was a wanted man. She knew I committed the murders, so she didn't need the name to tie me to them.

"I'm not telling you my name," I snapped.

"Fuck off, then," she bit back as she turned away from me.

I leaned over, grabbed her chin, and craned her neck, forcing her to look at me. She flashed hazel eyes at me that made my heart skip a beat, which I didn't even think was possible at that point in my life. At my lowest of lows.

"Don't talk to me like that, little girl."

She tensed her jaw, and her eyes hardened. "I'm not a little girl," she said. "I have a job. A career. An education." She scoffed. "And I *help* people instead of *killing* them."

Fuck. Her.

I once had a career. I was a researcher for the state. I had a master's degree. Hell, I used to help people too. I was once more than the man holding a rough grasp around that girl's chin. My hand left her face and made contact with the couch behind her head. She flinched. I wasn't going to hit her, especially when she was being . . . well, truthful.

I stood and dragged her off the couch, but she planted her heels, refusing to let me take her another step. "Fuck you." I snarled my words at her, hurling them with venom. She didn't deserve it, but she was the embodiment of everything my ex-wife thought of me. She also thought I was an utter failure. I might as well have been a murderer back then because to her, I axed our marriage.

There was nothing on Vanessa's face that made me think she wanted what I was going to do. But I couldn't stop the desire to do it. It wasn't the devil on my shoulder. No. It was the devil inside me.

I leaned in and kissed her, hard and heavy. I ran my hands up the soft skin of her neck and wrapped them around it. She was against my body, leaning in enough to encourage me to go further.

She let me inside her mouth, and my tongue explored hers. She tasted like she hated me, but I didn't care. Her hands pushed against my chest, as if she finally felt the weight of what was happening. I didn't want to pull away, even as her hands pushed against me. Her lips tightened. She wanted me off her mouth.

The devil in me roared to keep going.

I stopped, drawing away from her. She pulled back her hand and slapped me. Slapped the ever-loving holy hell out of me. It rattled me where the pain in my head still ripped through my brain.

"You're a killer," she said. She put her hand to her mouth as if she could wipe me from her lips.

"I'm sorry about your arm," I said as I tried to calm my

breaths. I left her in the kitchen. I had nothing more to say. There was no rebuttal.

I was a killer.

I took pain relievers with a mouthful of faucet water and leaned against the counter as a pang of hunger squeezed my gut. I couldn't remember my last meal, but based on the contents of my vomit, it had been too long. The crackers I nibbled were not enough sustenance.

Vanessa came into the kitchen and leaned against the doorway. She looked at the bottle of ibuprofen on the counter. "Did you eat with those?"

"No," I said with a shrug.

She went to the fridge and poured a glass of milk, handing it to me so forcefully that it dribbled over the rim. "Drink. You'll get an ulcer if you don't."

"Yes ma'am."

"That's even worse than calling me a little girl," she said with a curl of her lip. "I'm not a little girl, but I'm certainly no ma'am either."

There was a knock on the door, and both of our heads swiveled to the front of the house. I slunk along the wall and peered out the window. I wasn't imagining the cops that time. There were no flashing lights or sirens blaring, but they were there. For sure. I reached for the gun tucked into my waistband.

"Go," she commanded.

Where? Where the fuck was I supposed to go?

"Don't say anything stupid, Vanessa, because I'm not going to prison." I gestured toward the pistol at the curve of my back. I crept around the corner, obscured by the wall separating the living room from the long hallway leading toward the rustic bedrooms. I could hear everything.

45

Vanessa's soft footfalls. The twist of the lock, then the doorknob.

"Morning," she greeted the officer.

"Good morning," two voices said in unison. Not just an officer. Officers. I imagined them peering in, looking around the quaint house tucked into the middle of fucking nowhere. "Sorry to bother you, ma'am, but have you seen anyone or heard anything strange within the last few days?"

I smirked when he called her ma'am, because I knew it irritated her. I imagined the tick of her jaw when he said it.

"Gosh, you know, I work a lot. I don't know that I would have been home enough to see or hear anything," she said with a laugh.

"Are you okay?" a deep voice asked. I wondered if she was playing me, giving them messages without words. A tilt of her head my way, a nervous blink, anything that would give me up. If she did, their deaths would be on her hands, and I'd let her live so she could feel the weight of that guilt.

Don't be stupid, little girl.

"Do I not look okay?" she asked. "Back-to-back shifts will do that."

I peered over the wall. She was brushing her hair down, and she'd thrown a sweater on to cover her bruise.

Good girl.

"Nurse?"

"Is it that obvious?"

"No, we saw the decal on the back of your car. My wife works in the NICU," the deep voice said.

"Bless her. I don't know that I could do that job. Well, if that's all, I'll take a card if you'd like. In case I see anything."

There was a long pause. He was assessing her, reading

her body language. I couldn't imagine it was all that great. She did just have a homicidal man's tongue in her mouth.

"Do you mind if we come in to look around? Just to make sure you're safe."

I expected her to welcome them in, let them find me organically. I pulled out the gun, switching the safety off as I let it fall to my side. I'd shoot my way out of there if I had to.

"I really don't think that's necessary. I just settled down to get some sleep, and I'm seriously on the verge of crashing. Ask your wife how she feels after doubles." Her voice drew up in annoyance at the end.

"She's miserable, I can tell you that." The officer laughed.

"If you leave a card, I promise to call if I see *anything*," Vanessa said.

"Here's my card. Call me if you notice anything out of the ordinary."

"Absolutely. Thank you, officers."

The door slammed, and I peered out from my hiding place. She was breathless with her back against the wall. She shrugged off her sweater, fanning herself to try to calm down. Her eyes widened when she saw the gun in my hand. I flipped the safety on and tucked it behind me again. I walked over to her, putting my hands out until they rested on either side of her head. She chewed on her bottom lip.

"Why'd you protect me?" I asked.

Her lips tightened and her eyebrows furrowed. "I protected myself. I'm harboring a fucking killer."

"You did so good," I praised. I leaned in and kissed her forehead.

She squirmed against my touch. "Don't," she said as she pushed my arm away and walked off.

I kind of liked getting her going, the way her cheeks flushed red and her eyes took on a darker shade of green.

I had no idea why she lied for me, but I was fucking glad she did.

CHAPTER 7

I pressed my forehead against the handle of the refrigerator. My head throbbed. My stomach ached. I couldn't sleep from the pain. The anxiety. No amount of medication in the damn house could take the edge off the withdrawal.

"I told you, you need a hospital," Vanessa said as she came up behind me, yawning as she leaned against the wall. I must have woken her up with the light.

"And I told *you* I can't go to the hospital."

"This is unethical." She snatched something off the island, pushed me aside, and grabbed my chin, forcing me to look at her. A bright light flashed in front of my eyes. "Your pupils look better than they did. Has your vision cleared up?"

"Yes," I told her with a groan as I dropped my head back.

She prodded at my cheeks and forehead before grabbing my wrist and wrapping a hand around it to check my pulse. "You're diaphoretic. Tachycardic."

"I don't know what any of that means, doc, but

thanks." I drew away from her touch and sat at the island. The same one I imagined bending her over. My dick was drowning in withdrawal too and had no interest in playing. "I need more than this over-the-counter shit," I groaned as I dropped my head into my trembling hand.

"You're an addict. That's all you need to take."

I glanced at her. "I'm not an addict like *that.*"

"Your body tells me that's a big fat lie," she quipped as she pulled a loaf of bread out of the cabinet.

"I got addicted to drugs because my life went to shit," I whispered.

"And that helped your life be less shitty, huh?" She gestured toward my hand, reminding me of the murders.

So sassy.

I was in no mood for it.

I swallowed. I was locked in the memory of the day I found out my wife was having an affair. It was a Tuesday, and I had come home from work to surprise her for lunch. What I found was our fucking neighbor having her for a meal instead. I could only focus on his hand on her bare chest, which was stupid because he was balls deep inside her, but it was his big hand on her chest that got me. She hadn't let me see her with her shirt off in two years, and there she was, laid out in front of him while he got to touch the tits I hadn't gotten to see in so long.

So what'd I do? I turned around and went back to work. I did a double shift, avoiding the problem and burying myself in my work like he buried himself inside her.

I still remember her scrambling words as I left. "*Cole, stop! Wait!*" There was no point staying to hear her excuses, because my heart had already shattered.

I looked up at Vanessa. "The drugs made it feel less . . . real."

"What?"

I looked down at my hands as she made a sandwich on the counter. "My life. It made it hurt less. My marriage fell apart, and my job soon after. Then my home, which wasn't even one any longer." I had no clue why I poured my life out between us for her to use against me. I would blame the withdrawal for my loose lips. It was the only thing that made sense.

"I thought drugs ruined your marriage," she said as she plopped a plate down in front of me. "Eat." She sat down with her own sandwich and stared at me as she ate.

"No. My job ruined my marriage, ironically. And then she was unfaithful." I took a bite of the sandwich. It was flavorless, and its mere existence turned my stomach.

"Shit," she exhaled. "How'd you find out?"

"I walked in."

"*Shit.*" She shook her head. "That's rough."

"It's not an excuse for becoming addicted to drugs and committing a double homicide." I sneered at myself. I knew that. It was a really poor coping mechanism, but at the time, it numbed the hurt enough to talk me off the literal and figurative ledge.

"Or breaking into someone's home. Assaulting them. Forcing them to take care of you," she said as she finished the last bite of her sandwich. There was a twitch in the corners of her lips that contradicted her tone.

"Fair," I responded. She was right. "I didn't really *assault* you." *Not outside of my head, at least.*

"You hit me. And this." She lifted her sleeve to showcase the bruise on her arm.

I tightened my lips. I had apologized for both injuries. I just had to keep her from running away.

I stood and walked behind her. Goosebumps rose on

her skin from my presence, and fear brushed along her flesh. I rubbed my hand over the bruise. "I didn't want to hurt you."

"Don't," she said.

"Who's the guy in the picture in your wallet?" Her scent wafted up to me, the sweet scent of strawberry.

"Wh-what?"

I grabbed her purse off the ottoman in the living room, drew out her wallet, and flipped it open to the picture tucked into the pocket. The one I noticed when I was ransacking her purse earlier. "Him."

She swallowed. "My boyfriend." A rosy hue painted her cheeks.

A pang of jealousy teased my stomach. I kept imagining how it'd feel inside her, and he got to feel what she felt like. She looked like she'd be tight. She sounded like her moans would be fucking mind bending. Fuck. My dick ignored the pain in every other inch of my body, springing to life and pressing against my jeans.

A single tear slid down her cheek.

"What's wrong, little girl?" I brushed her hair back, and she flinched from my touch.

"He passed away last year in a car wreck." Her gaze dropped along with her shoulders. "He was driving here to spend winter break with me."

"I'm sorry . . ." I whispered, closing her wallet and pushing it aside.

"Don't. I don't need your sympathy. And stop calling me little girl." Her voice rose at the end, anger masking her sadness.

I gripped her chin and lifted it. "Or what? What will you do if I keep calling you little girl?"

She exhaled a sharp breath. "Fuck you, dude. Honestly.

I don't even understand what the fuck this is! You break into my house. You hold me hostage. What's your exit—"

I kissed her, shutting up the flurry of words racing from her lips. She put her hands up to my chest, pushing at me as her cheeks puffed out in frustration. I kept my mouth on hers until the anger coursed through her and she became too warm with heat and I had to pull away.

I smirked at her as she stared at me. "Fuck you," she hissed. She started to walk away. When she reached the shadow of the doorway, she turned back to me. "Don't do that again."

No promises.

CHAPTER 8

The steam swirled around the bathroom, filling every inch of it with the billowing vapors as the hot water embraced my tired body. It felt incredible. I was getting better by the day, and I'd actually gotten a little sleep. I inhaled the strawberry-scented shampoo in my hand before rubbing it through my hair. It smelled like her. Red-tinged water swirled around the drain as I finally washed my crimes away from my skin. I'd been too phobic to shower, preferring to live in the skin of the monster I had become. It wouldn't ease what I did, but it was nice to cleanse myself.

The best part? I had nightmares of the murders when I slept, which meant I was showing signs of humanity again —a blessing and a curse. I could feel it. It forced me to confront all that I became. What I deserved to remember for the rest of my life.

I never wanted to forget the two people I killed. I wanted them to sully my memory every day that I lived and they didn't.

I turned off the water, wrapped a towel around my waist, and stood in front of the sink. The steam wrapped around me like a warm, wet hug. I wiped it away from the mirror, confronting my sober self for the first time in quite a while. This face looked more familiar than any of the other reflections that stared back at me in the last several months. The bloodshot eyes were fading and becoming my own again.

I walked into the hallway, and a cool gust of air blew up from the old hardwood floors. When I entered the bedroom, a folded pair of jeans and a shirt waited on the bed. Her father's, if I had to guess based on the style.

The jeans hung a little loose on my hips, and the tie-dyed sleeveless t-shirt was horrendous. I wasn't sure what was worse, my crime or that fucking shirt. I was ten years older the moment it hit my skin. I looked like a dad.

Vanessa's lips crept upward when she saw me. Even though I had muscles that worked for that type of shirt, I looked ridiculous.

"Lookin' real stylish," she said before returning her attention to the book in her lap. Reading a book? What a mundane thing to do with a killer in your home. I peered over her shoulder to see what she was reading. A goddamn medical book. I snatched it from her hand, and she pouted. "I have my certification exam soon," she said as she reached for it. "Assuming I'll be alive for it."

"When was the last time you had a day off before I came here?"

She twisted her mouth. "A while. But I'd rather be at work than held hostage."

"So . . . you just work and study?"

Her eyes narrowed. "Pardon me for not having the time to get addicted to drugs and commit felonies." Shots fired. And they kind of hit.

I tossed her book beside her and left her alone in the

living room. I wasn't giving her shit for working hard. Believe me, I wouldn't. But also, she was twenty-two and lived like that was all she was born to do. Me coming around was probably one of the few breaks she'd had in a while. Maybe something good could come from it. Maybe she would realize she could do more than work and study. She didn't need to repeat all I'd done—in fact, I'd suggest she didn't—but maybe a few steps on my path would benefit her. Just not the whole journey.

Her hand touched my shoulder, and I turned toward her. Her lip jutted out, like she felt bad. As she should have. That was a low blow.

"I'm sorry," she whispered.

"I don't need your apology, little girl." I walked to the cabinet, pulled out a glass, and filled it with water. I gulped it down. "I got addicted to drugs and committed several felonies."

I turned my gaze to her, and she gave me a pinched smile. She was fighting a real one, though. I set the glass on the counter, and a drop of water dripped from the rim and cascaded down the smooth exterior.

With the confidence only a tie-dyed dad shirt could give, I walked into her and took her face in my hands. I kissed her. She relaxed into my touch for only a moment, squeezing the fabric of my shirt between loose hands. I pulled away from her, and her eyes gleamed an intense shade of green. I couldn't tell if she wanted me to keep going or if she wanted to smack me again.

She shook her head. "No," she whispered, and it was the most unconvincing fucking no I'd ever heard. But I respected it. "This cannot happen." She gestured between us.

"Not even out of convenience?"

"Especially not out of that. We're both lonely and trapped in here right now, but it doesn't give me free rein to throw my morals out the window. Yours are already long gone, clearly." She flashed a playful glare at me.

"Fair point. If you change your mind, you know where to find me."

"I won't," she said with a firmness that seemed like it was more for her than me.

I tapped the doorframe. Her resolve was weakening, and it shifted my fantasies. It went from wanting to force her for my pleasure to forcing her for hers. I ached to make her come.

I had no clue what would happen to me once I left there. She was letting me stay, and I had no idea why. It couldn't be for long, though. I had to get out of the area, somewhere far away from the scene that was still making headlines in the news.

I sat in the recliner, kicking my feet up as I watched the reporter talking on the television. I turned the channel, avoiding the news and hiding from the reality beyond these walls.

Vanessa came closer and grabbed my hand. She examined the slash on my palm. Her fingers prodded at the Steri-Strips, making sure they were still adhered. "It doesn't look infected, which is surprising. Make sure you pat them dry, don't rub."

"Got it, doc," I said before drawing my hand from her soft, warm grasp.

She rolled her eyes, went to the couch, curled up with her legs beneath her, and lifted her book. The way she got lost in her work reminded me so much of myself. Well, how I used to be. I had no clue what I'd do once I left and confronted the real world that never stopped spinning, even when I pretended it had. I only knew I had no intention of going back to drugs. I'd gotten through the worst parts of my withdrawal, and the twist in my stomach was lessening by the hour. My mind was already clearer. Not crystal, but close. It would be a while before I felt like the person I was before the drugs, but part of me wasn't sure I wanted to be *that* person again. I didn't know if the devil still remained in my mind or if he left to find someone else desperate enough to let him inside.

I needed something between work-obsessed and weak-and-drug-addicted and fearless. Some nice happy medium. Somewhere in the middle of boredom and chaos. Something kind of like this goddamn shirt.

CHAPTER 9

Vanessa had to work, and I had to let her go. I had to
trust she'd come back without a police escort. It was
a long shot that she wouldn't betray me. I'd have probably
betrayed me by now. So I waited. And waited.

Twelve hours is a really long time when you're waiting
to see if someone will return . . . alone. The rare headlight
that glinted against the window made me tense as I
anticipated the flash of red and blue police lights.

I went into her bedroom and thumbed through her
stuff again, spritzing a bit of her scent around me. I rifled
through her panty drawer, sat on the bed, and lay back as
my fingers entwined with the black silk fabric of a pair of
her panties. I was uncomfortably hard at the thought of her
wearing them. My cock throbbed.

I pulled myself out of my jeans and went to stroke
myself. She told me not to rub at the Steri-Strips on my
hand, but that's precisely what I wanted to do. I wrapped
my left hand around my cock, and it felt like a stranger's
hand as I stroked up my length. Jerking off with your non-
dominant hand was shit. My movements were jerky and

uncoordinated. I wrapped the silk around my cock and made long, slow strokes with my right hand. Yeah, I was still rubbing, but my hand glided more easily along the silk. Remember that happy medium I was trying to find? That would have to be it.

I dropped my head back and let a soft groan leave my lips as I stroked myself. The head of my cock was sensitive against the soft fabric. My thoughts went right to Vanessa. Inappropriate thoughts that still hovered on force, which disturbed me. I was sober and mostly caught up on sleep, yet I still thought about her sweet whimpers and pleas as I spread her open. I stroked myself until the pleasure rose from my balls and spilled onto the black fabric. It was at that moment that I realized why I wanted to force her, and it had nothing to do with feeling the need to sink inside her. Disgust laced her pleas in every fantasy I'd had—the way she couldn't look me in the eye as I took her.

It was how I felt about myself.

Well, shit.

A sharp inhale snapped my attention to the door. Vanessa was in the doorway. I could only imagine what I looked like with my spent cock beneath her panties. Jesus.

She backpedaled into the shadowy hallway.

I got out of bed and chased after her, zipping up my pants as I ran. I tossed her underwear in the garbage before slipping into the hall. "Vanessa?"

I found her in the kitchen, but she refused to look at me. Which was fair. I wasn't sure I'd look at myself, either. I had *never* jerked off into anyone's underwear in my life. Fuck if I knew why I felt the need to do it with hers.

"About that . . ." I whispered.

"I don't even want to acknowledge what I just saw," she said with a quick wave of her hand.

"But—"

"Don't. I didn't turn you in. Stupidly. I came home and found you invading every ounce of my privacy." Her eyes finally rose to meet mine. "You're disgusting. Vile."

"I love how this is inciting more emotion from you than me being a murderer."

She clenched her hands at her sides. "Because you . . . you . . ." She exhaled sharply, and it blew hair off her forehead. She was too angry to even form the concise sentence she needed.

"Stop, little girl. Just stop." I stepped into her, ignoring the red flush of her cheeks and the daggers she shot at me with her intense green eyes.

"Don't fucking call me that!" She pushed at my chest. "Fuck you."

I took a step back, letting her think she was strong enough to make me do so. Her blue scrubs were stained, and she looked tired. She probably wanted to come home, shower, and change out of her work clothes. Instead, she found me pleasing myself to thoughts of her. I understood her outrage. I had taken things to a really weird level.

Vanessa pushed past me and went to the bathroom while I sat in the chair and picked at the strips on my hand. The edges were peeling away, probably because I rubbed instead of dabbed. They were still holding, though, and that's all that mattered.

When she came out in pajamas, with her wet hair clinging to her neck, she still avoided my gaze as if I was the murderer she probably should have avoided from the beginning. Any rapport I'd built with her was gone, thrown away like her used and discarded panties.

"You can take the bedroom," I told her as I moved toward the couch.

"What were you thinking about?" Her eyes snapped to me, boring into me and taking me off guard.

"Why the hell does it matter, little girl?" I scoffed. Her lips tightened. She *hated* being called that. Why did I enjoy it so much?

Her eyes narrowed like she was trying to figure out why it mattered to her. "Forget it," she said, realizing the path she'd incidentally taken toward me.

No, I wouldn't just forget it. I wanted to know why her cheeks were still so rosy. Was it the warm water of her shower or was it something else? Something worse?

I backed her against the wall, and a picture frame rattled above her head as her body met the drywall. "Tell me why you want to know."

She swallowed hard, and her expression tightened. Her body became rigid and defensive, and she looked like she wanted to punch me in the face, which I probably deserved. But when her muscle twitched in her right arm, I reached out and pinned her wrist to the wall.

"Don't try to hit me, Vanessa," I said with a sneer. My body pressed against hers and responded to her heat. My free hand left the wall and nestled beneath her jaw, lifting her onto the tips of her toes as I gripped her neck. She whimpered. The sound went straight to my goddamn dick. "I know you're thinking about it. Are you thinking about kneeing me in the balls or reaching for the gun?"

She shook her head. Well, tried to. She wasn't looking at me with the proper fear she should have felt. There was a hint of a flirt in the flutter of her eyelashes. I lowered her until she could stand flat-footed and leaned into her, hovering inches from her face. She smelled like strawberry, the scent that got me hard the instant I got a whiff of it. I grabbed her other wrist and pinned it above her head. Her back arched against the wall.

"I don't want you to kill me," she whispered, her lips so close to mine. The arteries in her neck pulsed in time with her heartbeat. "Are you going to? I mean, when it's all said and done?"

Why the fuck would I tell her if I was? And why the double fuck would I tell her if I had any chance of getting laid first? But no, I had no intention of killing her.

"No, little girl, I won't. Unless you do something fucking stupid." I adjusted her wrists so I could hold them both in one hand and let my free hand roam down her face. I ran my finger along her lower lip, which was set in a pout.

Her breath rolled over mine, and the heat of her cheeks crept down and mottled her chest. The blush stopped at the swells of her breasts. Fuck me.

"What's your name?" she asked through a sobering breath.

"Don't ask me that," I snarled. She flinched, and I softened my expression a little. "You know I can't tell you that."

She nodded as if she understood the gravity of what she'd hold if I gave her my name. From what I could tell, the police had jack shit for suspects, and I didn't want her to be able to put a name to one.

"Let me go," she whispered, dropping her gaze from mine. The words made my cock swell until it pressed painfully against the zipper of my jeans. I fought the urge to reach down and adjust myself.

"When you say that, it does something wicked to me, little girl," I groaned. "Do you really want to know what I was thinking about earlier?"

She swallowed before letting out a small nod.

"I was thinking about laying you down and spreading your legs." I considered stopping there because she was so heated with confused anger. "But I didn't want you to want it."

Her eyebrows furrowed. "Wait. You thought about forcing me to fuck you?" Her lip curled, but then her expression flattened.

"More times than I care to admit. And I'm sorry I'm not more sorry about that."

She drew her legs together. It was either from fear . . . or excitement. Or fear because she was excited. "Why haven't you?"

Her question made *my* eyebrows furrow that time. What a question. Probably a fucking trap. I didn't answer her. I couldn't, because I didn't really have an answer.

I took the risk and let my hand roam further down her body until I reached the heat between her legs. When she kept her thighs pinched together, I dropped her wrists and leaned into her as I forced her legs open with a rough grasp. When I had them far enough apart, I stuck my knee between them, keeping her open for me. She pushed her hands into my chest, but the way she gripped my shirt at the end of every shove nulled her actions. I pinned her harder against the wall until she lost the space she needed to push me away. My hand rode up her thigh, where a red mark from my grasp branded her pale skin.

"Don't," she whispered. The way she said it, I believed she wanted me to stop. I fully believed that. She wanted me to stop. But there was something in her that wanted me to ignore it. I knew it the moment I moved the crotch of her shorts aside and rubbed a finger along her slick pussy.

"I'm sorry, but I need you," I growled as I sank my

fingers inside her, making a come-worthy whimper leave her lips. "And I think you need me."

I fucked her with my fingers until she spasmed around them. I wanted it to be my goddamn cock more than I wanted meth when I was withdrawing. She dug her fingers into my arms as I quickened the motion.

"Tell me you don't want it," I growled into her ear.

"I don't want you." Again, her voice was rich with what she believed. She didn't want me. She wanted the pleasure I was giving her, though.

I pulled her over to the island, but instead of undressing her like in my fantasy, I pushed her chest onto the granite. I fisted her hair as I craned her neck, eliciting a true whimper. The kind that made me throb.

She put her arms back and tried to push me away from her. "Please, stop." Her words were gritty between clenched teeth.

I should have stopped. Tears glossed her eyes, and it was a real display of her angst over what I was doing to her. But she didn't flail nearly hard enough. Didn't fight me enough to make me think I couldn't push her through her protest. I pressed my cock against her ass, with only the fabric of my jeans and her shorts between us. If she needed to tell me no to make herself feel better about fucking me, I'd let her.

The sound of my falling zipper echoed over her whimpers and soft pleas. I knew she didn't want me inside her as I pulled my cock out and rubbed it between her legs. She tried to close her thighs, but I kicked them open and jammed my knee between them once more.

"Shh," I whispered as I pulled her shorts aside and pushed myself inside her.

Heaven. She felt like fucking heaven. Even better than my fantasies. I pulled her head back and wiped the tear from her cheek. "Don't cry, little girl," I said as I thrust into her, spreading the salty bead across her face. I worried I'd lose my erection as her rigid body made me second guess it all. Was she indulging in my fantasy, maybe even her own, or was I ruining her?

I lifted her chest and rubbed my hand over her soft, round belly. She was so goddamn curvy. And fucking angelic. My hand rose beneath her shirt and went to her chest. "I know you enough to know I wouldn't be able to get this close to you if you didn't want to let me inside you," I growled into her ear before biting her neck.

"Fuck you," she hissed.

I responded to her harsh words with harsher thrusts, the strength behind them rattling the island in front of her. The glasses trembled on the granite. "You wouldn't be dripping down your thighs if you didn't want it. I wouldn't have been able to push inside you so easily if you weren't so goddamn wet." My words tightened her expression. She trembled but I wasn't sure why. Excitement? Anger? "Touch yourself," I said. She shook her head. "Touch yourself, and I'll stop once I make you come."

"I can't," she whined.

I grabbed her hand and put it against her pussy. "You can."

She strained her neck against my hand wrapped in her hair as she rubbed between her legs. Her body melted for a few moments before tensing once more, but for another reason. I fucked her, jerking her head back with every unwavering thrust. Tears continued falling down her cheeks, as if the guilt overflowed from her. Guilt from her body tightening around me like it was.

I groaned as she spasmed around me, squeezing the shaft of my dick almost painfully. "Good girl," I whispered as I stopped thrusting and let myself bathe in her spasms, which were trying to draw my come from my cock. Whether she intended to or not. "Come on my cock," I said as I pushed into her with long and deep thrusts that let me feel every ebb and flow of her walls around my dick.

She moaned and tried to stifle the sound as she came. She clenched around me so hard I thought she'd push me out of her. I held her hips to keep myself balls deep inside her as tremors vibrated through her body.

"Don't come inside me," she whispered as her pleasure subsided.

I struggled with the desire to fill her up as my pleasure crawled toward the head of my dick. I was going to come inside her one way or another. "Your mouth or your pussy?"

She groaned. "My mouth."

I pulled out of her, admiring her come on my dick. Her excitement coated me, and it was worth every moment of her possibly hating me after it.

I kept my hand in her hair as I guided her to her knees. The moment her green eyes rolled up to me, I had to stroke myself. She was the most stunning thing on her knees. I'd tell her later, but I *needed* to unload inside her right then. Nothing else mattered as I pushed my cock past her full lips. I ignored the tears that slipped past the creases of her eyes as she sucked me off.

"I'm going to come." I grabbed the back of her head and held her in front of me as I pulsed my hips against her mouth, coming down her throat. She gagged before swallowing. "Fuck," I groaned as I pulled out of her mouth.

My cock was spent in front of her face, and she just looked . . . I didn't even know how to describe it. She looked like she wasn't angry. Not scared. Satiated, maybe? I helped her to her feet, and she looked at me with doe eyes.

I brushed her hair from her face, and she didn't flinch that time. I wiped the tears from her cheeks. "Cole," I told her with a tight smile. "My name's Cole."

It was fucking stupid. I should have lied and told her another name. But the way she looked at me compelled me to tell her the truth.

Who I was.

I kissed her, tasting the sweetness of her pussy and the saltiness of my come as I slipped my tongue into her mouth. She kissed me back. "I'm sorry," I said as I stepped away from her, pulling back from what I wanted to draw closer to.

It would be absolutely fucking insane to fall for the damsel I put in distress.

CHAPTER 10

I woke up from one of my many nightmares, but I couldn't tell reality from my imaginings. The anguish was all very real as it choked me in my sleep. I felt the stabbing pain and the fear the couple felt. Sweat coated my skin as I snapped awake with panicked breaths. I had nightmares almost every night—bits and pieces of what I'd done. What I could remember, at least. It horrified me to know what I'd allowed myself to become.

When I walked into the kitchen, Vanessa was washing dishes, soaking the bottom of her shirt as she scrubbed with an edge of frustration. She wouldn't speak to me or even look me in the eye. A plate slipped from her hand and shattered against the steel sink.

"Fucking A," she said. An onslaught of whispered words left her lips, too low for me to hear. I took a step toward her as she grabbed a towel from the counter and wrapped it around her hand. A thick drop of blood fell down her pale arm, then a thicker line fell from beneath the towel.

I crossed the kitchen and stepped into her, reaching for her hand. She tugged it away from me, wincing against the movement.

"Let me see it," I said as I reached for her again.

"Don't touch me," she snapped back, still avoiding my eyes. "I'm fine!" Her icy words froze me in place.

I stood for a moment, respecting her space. The only thing that could cause the ice on her tongue was what I'd done to her last night. And while it made me feel bad, it was worth her anger to have felt her coming around my dick. That was the worst part. If I got to sink into her one time, it was better than a longing so deep it made my blood run cold. Made me mad with desire. Somehow it intoxicated me more than any drug. And even as she finally met my gaze with a fiery stare that burned me, I didn't regret it.

The blood slid down her arm and dripped in fat drops onto the hardwood floors beneath her. Her eyes welled with frustrated tears. "Fuck," she said, slow and drawn out.

"Give me your hand, little girl," I commanded, throwing the fire right back at her. I wasn't playing now. She was bleeding like a motherfucker.

Her eyes rounded and her shoulders deflated in defeat. She gave me her hand, and I unwrapped the saturated towel. She had sliced the hell out of herself, and she whimpered as I touched the tissue spreading in a frayed line along her palm. The irony wasn't lost on me. As my palm was healing, hers was split wide open. I had wanted to see her blood drip from her in one of my fantasies, but I didn't want that now.

I had no clue how to fix her wound, not like she knew how to tend to mine. She needed a doctor. It would be the best thing for her.

"You need to go to the hospital," I told her.

She shook her head furiously. "No fucking way."

My eyebrows furrowed. "Why the hell not?"

"Nurses are horrible patients, and I'm not going to my place of work with a cut on my hand."

As I watched the channel of her skin fill with more blood, I tightened my lips. "This is more than just a cut, little girl. I'll drive you." My stomach tightened. The thought of getting in that car and driving her into the city made my heart skip beats as it panicked in my chest. I'd take her, though. It was the least I could do.

Her green eyes shot up and narrowed. "I'm not going."

"Fuck, you're stubborn," I said. I wrapped her hand again and squeezed, putting pressure on it. I respected it, but it was real fucking stupid. If I ended up dead from my cut or some post infection, I would have deserved every bit of pain before the devil welcomed me into hell. But her? She didn't deserve that fate.

I dragged her toward the bathroom and rifled through the cabinet until I found the alcohol and Steri-Strips. When I set them on the countertop, I looked to her for directions. I put firm pressure on her hand, checking every so often to see if the bleeding had finally stopped. She leaned against the sink, and I sat on the closed toilet, keeping pressure on her wound. A suffocating silence hung between us.

"Are you going to tell me why you're so upset?" I asked. It was kind of a dumb question, but I wanted to hear her say it. That I assaulted her. Hurt her. That she hated me. I deserved that and more.

"Fuck you, Cole," she bit back.

I stood up, still clutching her hand. I towered over her, and her eyes rode up my body until they settled on my face.

73

"Watch your mouth, little girl." When I tugged the towel away a final time, the blood had settled within her wound, clotting nicely. "Tell me what to do," I whispered.

"Clean it with the alcohol."

I remembered the pain when she cleaned mine with the same fiery liquid. It was maddening. And she was already angry.

I put her hand over the sink and unscrewed the cap from the bottle. She took a sharp breath before I even began to pour it, anticipating the pain. I tipped the bottle over her hand, and the alcohol hit her wound. Old blood tinged the liquid pink as it swirled around the drain, and a deeper red left a darker tinge as fresh bleeding began once more. She bit her lower lip, trying to keep from screaming as her cheeks flamed red. She took it better than I had.

"Breathe," I said. She took a long breath, shivering with pain. I lifted her hand toward my mouth and softly blew on her cut—a long and slow exhale of breath that made her jaw tick.

She walked me through applying Steri-Strips to her cut. After closing it as best I could, I cleaned up the mess in the bathroom, slamming cabinets closed when I finished. When I turned back to her, I moved her against the wall and took her face between my hands, still stained with her blood.

"Tell me what's the matter with you," I commanded. I left no room for her to argue back.

"Please don't," she whispered. Her breath hitched. Her words made me twitch, and she knew it.

"What'd I tell you about those words, little girl?" I growled.

Her eyes rolled up to me in a sensual glare that confused the fuck out of me. She wanted more, I was fairly certain of that, but anger melded with her desire until I couldn't tell what she felt. It could easily have been both. Her desire made her angry.

I took a leap of faith and slipped my hand beneath the waistband of her shorts. She gasped as my fingers grazed her pussy. She was so goddamn wet. I pulled away from her, hooked my fingers into the waistband, and tugged her shorts down her thick, pale thighs. She pushed at me with her uninjured hand. Even with both hands, she couldn't have derailed what I wanted to do to her. With one? She was helplessly mine.

"Cole, don't," she said more firmly as I dropped to my knees in front of her. She fought harder, her injured hand clenching into a fist and making her wince. Despite her punching at my shoulder and trying to push me away, I leaned into her and buried my tongue between her legs. "I don't want this!" she cried out with a frustrated strain in her voice.

"Just let me make you come," I whispered against her skin. "Stop fighting me." I was sick of her assaults on my shoulder and head, even if it was futile and weak.

She tasted fucking incredible. I licked in long strokes, curling my tongue along her clit. I flicked it with the tip of my tongue before going back to the long strokes that made her pelvis tilt into my face. Her hand rested on my shoulder instead of hitting it. She fought her moans and the pleasure I gave her. She could pretend to hate it all she wanted, but her body begged for more, swelling and tilting until she spread open for me.

I buried my face deeper in her pussy as I sucked on her clit. Once I slipped my fingers inside her, she was done for. Her thighs quivered and her hand left my shoulder to grab a fistful of my hair. She tugged hard, and it wasn't just from pleasure. She was still riding the coattails of her anger.

Whatever she felt, it made her pull me deeper into her pussy.

"Cole, I'm serious. St . . . op." Her words broke apart at the end. She was less and less convincing the more her body responded to my touch.

I pulled away and looked up at her. "Not until you come on my face. Come, and I'll leave your sweet pussy alone." I smirked at her. "Promise."

She groaned, but instead of arguing with me, she buried her hand in my hair again and shoved me between her legs. She would do anything to get me off her, even if it meant getting off from me.

She gripped the doorframe with her injured hand, leaving a smear of blood along the white paint. Her nails dug into the wood. She lost control of her moans, and it was music to my fucking ears.

She didn't like me, but right at that moment, she needed to. Her body needed the release.

I knew she wouldn't tell me when she was coming. She wouldn't give me that satisfaction. No, I had to grab her hip and grind my face against her soaked pussy until she shuddered against my mouth. She came, her pussy tightening around my fingers. I licked her with slow, broad strokes as she spasmed against my touch.

I stood up, half expecting her to hit me. But when she just stared at me with a horrified look on her face, I couldn't help but take her face in my hands and fucking kiss her. I spread her come along her chin as her lips parted and welcomed me inside her mouth.

Our kiss was full of hatred and anger, desire snaking through the emotions. For her. For me, it was all goddamn desire. She was the most addictive taste on my tongue. More than drugs. Far more than drugs.

I didn't know how she would feel once the pleasure melted away from her body and she remembered the man who was between her legs was the monster that forced his way into her home.

CHAPTER 11

The moment my eyes opened, the weight of the world sat on my chest. What I had done the night that brought me here still plagued me, even though who did *that* wasn't me. It was my body but it wasn't my mind, and it was definitely not my heart. It just wasn't who I was.

My eyes were still heavy with sleep, and I kept them closed as I thought about last night, wondering if it'd been a dream. I kicked off a blanket that wasn't there when I went to sleep, my skin becoming increasingly warm the more my thoughts wandered to Vanessa. I loved making her come. Loved how much she hated that I made her come.

I got out of bed and walked toward her bedroom. Her door was slightly ajar. Through the crack, I peered at her soft form beneath a blanket. The fabric of her purple sheets wrapped around her, but as she turned onto her belly in her sleep, it twisted, exposing her pale thigh and the cuffs of her ass.

Fuck me.

The red locks of her hair draped over the pillow, and my mind wandered to how it felt wrapped around my hand. I wanted to go into her room, yank down her panties, and spread her thighs as I drew her hips to mine. My cock twitched.

I went into the room and closed the door behind me. My breath hitched as I tried to stop myself from doing something incredibly fucking stupid. But I couldn't help myself. I wasn't sure how she'd react. I anticipated her struggle, but I hoped to feel her pleasure.

I crawled into bed with her, pinning her body with mine. The weight of me straddling her hips woke her up, a horrified yelp leaving her lips before I silenced her with my hand around her mouth.

There was fear. True fear.

When she got a glimpse of me, her screams became whimpers and her body relaxed a bit beneath me. The intensity of her fear washed away in front of me.

"Don't stop fighting me, little girl," I whispered against her ear.

She writhed beneath me. Her nostrils flared above my hand, and she flashed her green eyes at me. I reached down and unzipped my jeans, pulling my cock through the slit. I ripped her panties, and the tearing sound went right to my dick. More whimpers escaped through my fingers. She kept squirming beneath me, rubbing my warm cock against her ass. I reached down and pushed my cock inside her, and her warmth and wetness welcomed me.

I spread her open as I sat up on my knees and pulled her hips toward me. I fucked her mercilessly, with a hunger I should have stifled. But her soft, thick thighs were too inviting. The curves of her lower stomach were warm against my hand as I held her, and I squeezed the flesh as I thrust deep inside her, pulling out only to plunge further into her.

I dropped my hand from her mouth and ran it along the curve of her neck. I expected her to scream out obscenities and hatred toward me. But she was silent. Not even whimpers of pleasure escaped her throat, which was almost more eerie than if she had screamed out in anger.

I fucked her harder, until whimpers left her freed lips. I fisted her hair and pulled back, noticing the bite of her lip as I did.

I'm not a rapist. I'm not. She wanted me, but she couldn't get past her own morals to allow herself to welcome me inside her. I was a monster, and she wasn't willing to allow herself to play with one. The only way she could accept me was by force. But the desire beneath her objections let her subtle consent pass between us. As she leaned her chest deeper into the bed and lifted her hips for me, she told me all she needed to without a single word.

I slipped my hand between her legs and rubbed her swollen clit.

"Cole, don't," she whispered. I throbbed at her words. The moment I started to touch her, to please her, that was when guilt poured from her mouth. The guilt caused by making her come.

"Come," I growled. "You know how this works. Come, and I'll be quicker. I won't use you longer, no matter how fucking good you feel."

She jolted from my words. I went from circles around her clit to rubbing along the wet, slick hood of it. She buried her face in the pillow, trying to hide the sounds of her pleasure. She couldn't hide it, though, not as her thighs trembled when I leaned over her or as her pussy clenched around me.

"Good girl," I whispered. "Mouth or pussy?" I asked. She knew I wanted to fill one or the other. She knew the very first night I fucked her that I would come inside her, but it was her choice if she wanted me to spill it down her throat or push it deep into her pussy.

She didn't answer me with words, only backed her ass into me, pushing against my pelvis where the pleasure was too difficult to hold back. I kept a palm on her spasming clit as I fucked her, finishing deep inside her. I released a gravelly groan that made her sigh into the bedding.

I pulled out of her, my come dripping between her legs and falling onto the sheet. I rubbed my sensitive head along her equally sensitive clit before bringing her face to mine. She looked like she'd been crying. I never noticed.

I kissed her, pulling her into me. My come dripped down her thighs as she sat on her knees on the bed. "What are you feeling, little girl?" I asked as I held her away from my mouth, our chests heaving against each other.

She shook her head but leaned into me for another kiss. "Please don't ask me that," she said against my lips. Her forehead pressed against mine.

She knew all of this was wrong. I knew it was wrong. But fuck if it didn't feel like the rightest goddamn thing in the world. It felt right among all the wrong that we were hiding from.

I swiveled and sat on the bed, tugging her onto my lap. I didn't care if our come stained my pants. I just needed to feel her in my arms. She melted into me, which I didn't expect.

"I'm sorry, little girl," I whispered as I kissed the top of her head. She felt so small on my lap. So vulnerable.

I was sorry. I felt guilt for how I took her just then, mostly because she couldn't hint at me like she had before, not until I had already pushed inside her. When it would have been too late.

She stirred something primal inside me. I wanted nothing more than to please her and make her come as I selfishly took her. I'd never felt such things in my life, and I was almost certain she hadn't either.

We were living in some kind of dystopian reality where consent wasn't explicit; it was implied. I had to watch for her subtlest cues telling me she wanted more when her mouth said otherwise. It was a game of risk, teetering on the fine line between loving and hating what I did to her. And loving and hating me. But I had to push further and test the trust she had in me.

She was a new addiction, and I'd do more than murder to satiate the craving.

CHAPTER 12

I made breakfast for us, which felt like such a mundane thing to do, given the circumstances. The pattering water in the shower was the only sound, aside from the sizzle of bacon. My mind wandered with racing thoughts that merged together until I couldn't pull them apart. I felt every feeling I could feel, including the crawl beneath my skin that reminded me of how I felt when doing drugs.

I needed to know how she felt. I couldn't deal with her being so upset with herself. Or me. I hated the wall of discomfort that only seemed to fall when I fucked her, but the moment I pulled out of her or gave her pussy a final lick, it built right back up.

I heard the soft patter of her feet as she came into the kitchen, still quiet. I flipped off the burner and turned toward her. She was stunning. Her red hair was dark and wet against her neck, dampening the shoulder of her shirt. Black leggings clung to her thighs—the thighs I wanted against my head as I devoured her.

I stepped into her, expecting her to flinch or pull away from my touch, but she leaned into me instead. I took her face in my hands and lifted her gaze to mine. "I need you to tell me how you feel, little girl."

She didn't squirm about her nickname as her green eyes bored into mine. "I can't," she said with a shake of her head.

"Why not?"

Her posture was rigid and she was impossible to read. "Because I feel bad about it."

Fuck. I knew she was upset with me, and I knew I made mistakes, especially this morning. Hearing her say it, though . . . It was—

"Because I liked it," she whispered, drawing me out of the rush of self-loathing in my mind and silencing the doubt. I snapped my attention to her, dropping my hands from her cheeks to her neck. "And I hate that I liked it."

"I'm as torn as you are about why I feel such a need to make you come. I've never felt this way about anyone. It makes me do real stupid shit, like what happened in the bedroom. I didn't give you the chance to say a damn thing before I fucked you. I was selfish." I squeezed her, moving my hands up to grip the hair at the base of her neck. "And I'm sorry I don't feel worse about it, because you feel like home. You feel safe."

Her pale cheeks reddened. "No one has ever wanted me so badly. Needed to have me." She drew a sharp breath. "Went down on me like I was their last goddamn meal."

She was right. I needed her. "So why don't you let me please you? Let me bury my tongue or cock in your pussy instead of fighting me? Just let me make you feel good."

"Because I feel guilty. Even when you're getting me off, my stomach is twisting with guilt. I feel nauseated after I come because it shouldn't feel so good. You're a—"

"Don't finish your sentence, little girl. I know what I am. My guilt twists my stomach every day, and nightmares keep me up every night." I kissed her. My guilt vanished when I was inside her because it went into her, for her to harbor instead. "Is that why you've been so upset with me?" I asked.

She swallowed before nodding slowly. "I'm upset with myself," she whispered. "It all feels so wrong."

"I'm what's wrong, but what I do to you is right, little girl. You fight me because you hate that you feel *something* for me. It disgusts you. I disgust you. But there's something inside you that doesn't hate me. You want me to take you because if you *give* yourself to me, you're betraying all that you believe. Your morals say you shouldn't welcome a man like me inside you. That a guy like me is unsafe. Dangerous. And it's fucking true." I pulled one of my hands from behind her neck and brought it up to her warm, rosy cheeks. I rubbed her skin with my thumb. "I went too far this morning because I can't look at you without wanting to rip your clothes off."

Her lip quivered. The harshness in my tone contradicted the soft rub of her cheek beneath my thumb. When I saw the gloss in her eyes, I pulled her into my chest. I caused her anguish. I knew that. And I hated it.

"I'm going to leave tomorrow," I whispered before kissing the top of her head.

"But—" She stopped herself. Instead of saying anything else, she pressed herself against my chest, and I wrapped her up in my arms.

I didn't want to leave, but I had to. She would never let herself be with me, and every time I heard her moans and felt her orgasms, I became more reckless with riding that hair-thin line of consent. I would eventually make a mistake and take it too far. Make her hate me. I'd prove her right— the monster shouldn't have been welcomed inside her after all. Inside her sweet, clean home. Inside her trusting pussy. The one that ached for me as much as I ached for her didn't want a chaotic and dangerous man invited in. But there I was.

I had no idea where I would go, but I needed to leave while she still looked at me with some form of confused lust. While she was still intact.

"Go eat," I said as I pulled away from her.

We each grabbed a plate of bacon and eggs. She went to the couch to eat, and I hovered over the island counter. She turned on the goddamn news—the last thing I wanted to hear right then. I had enough on my mind without being reminded of all the evil out there, which included me.

When I finished my bacon, I looked over at Vanessa. Her mouth hung open, the reflection of the TV glistening in her wide eyes. I expected to see my face on the screen, to learn they'd finally linked me to my crime. When I walked into the living room and followed her stare to the television, my mouth hung open as well.

They showed the house and the pictures of my victims, but the whole tone of the report was different. Instead of headlines about finding their killer or learning what happened to them, it was about *them*. The victims. They showed clips of women being taken from the home, faces blurred.

Ten million worth of drugs found in the home. Women used for the transportation of drugs, rescued from a modified basement.

What. The. Fuck.

I looked at Vanessa, and she looked back at me. Neither of us could say a damn word. Not out loud, at least.

I committed murder, yes, but I killed a couple of goddamn drug lords. It didn't make me any less culpable, though. I would still end up on my knees in front of the devil one day, but it eased some of the guilt I held on to. And it didn't make me any less of a killer to Vanessa. I still took lives, and for that, I'd forever be the monster trying to get into her bed.

CHAPTER 13

I had to leave. The situation was always supposed to be temporary. It was a place to lay my weary head until everything blew over. I didn't expect it to be where I also laid my cock. Or a place where I laid out my vulnerabilities.

My failure as a husband.

Addiction.

The darkest secret I'd always have to hide.

How did that happen? Fuck if I knew, but I would do just about anything for her, including leaving. I had to. She was a shepherd, and I was the wolf in sheep's clothing she'd rescued. To be honest, I think she'd have saved me whether I dressed up as one of her flock or not. That's who she was, though. Someone much too good for me.

I walked into the kitchen, wearing a much quieter shirt of her father's and my freshly washed jeans. I found Vanessa on the couch, her nose buried in her book. My heart fluttered in my chest at the sight of her as her eyes traveled up my body. There was little conversation between us once I told her I was leaving, as if she didn't want to face the idea. She looked a bit betrayed. But I was older than her, and I had to be the responsible one, and *that* was the responsible thing to do.

I leaned over and put her face between my hands, and she rolled her eyes up to me. "I want to do something before I leave."

Vanessa cocked her head, her eyebrows furrowing in confusion. "What?" she asked as she folded the page and put the book beside her on the table. Her eyes rounded with sadness when she realized I said I was leaving. Maybe she thought I wasn't serious when I said I had to go. But I had to go.

I pulled a scarf from my pocket. "Go to the bedroom and put this over your eyes. Tie it tight."

"Wh-why?" she stammered.

"Just do it," I commanded, tugging her to her feet.

She hesitated, her eyes narrowing on me before she left me alone in the living room. I took a deep breath and listened to the loud tick of the songbird-faced clock on the wall. I followed her, expecting to find her in the bedroom but not blindfolded like I asked. I expected more of a fight. When I opened the door, she stood in the center of the room, her back toward the door and the scarf tied around her head. My cock swelled at the sight of her.

I walked behind her and she jumped as my breath hit the bare skin of her shoulder hidden only by the thin strap of a cami. I put my hand on her shoulder. "Shh, little girl," I whispered.

I adjusted her blindfold and tied it better behind her head.

"What are we doing?" she asked, lifting her chin to peek beneath the edge of the scarf. I circled her like a predator until I was face to face with her. Her lower lip quivered, pouted out a bit. I didn't know if it was from fear or excitement. I probably would be worried I was being prepared for my execution if I were her, but there she was, with slow, even breaths.

"I know you can't let yourself fuck me," I whispered. I took a step into her and began to unbutton her jeans. Her hand reached for my wrist to stop me. "This is what I mean." I grabbed her hand and put it at her side once more. I lowered the zipper, and the sound made me bite my lip. Her arm twitched, as if she wanted to stop me again. "Pretend I'm not me, little girl. And let me make you feel good before I go. I've fucked your willing body, but not that pretty mind of yours. I want both."

"Cole . . ." she whispered, a sternness in her hushed voice.

I didn't answer her. I wanted her to think I was anyone else.

Nameless.

Faceless.

Voiceless.

I'd be whoever she wanted me to be in her mind. Her late boyfriend? A goddamn celebrity? Anyone besides the person standing in front of her. Even though it hurt, I would be what she wanted, even though it wasn't me.

I pulled down her jeans, encouraging her as she put her hand on my shoulder and stepped out of them. My breath hitched at the sight of her black panties partially obscured by her thick thighs. I hungered for what was beneath them, but I wouldn't ravage her. I ran my hand up her shirt, hovering at the curves of her belly. Soft. Warm. I went higher, palming her stunning tits. I had to reach down and adjust myself the moment I got my hands on them. She inhaled sharply as I took off her shirt. She stood in front of me, wearing nothing more than those panties.

"What's happening?" she demanded once more.

I met her question with my mouth on her lips. That was the only answer she would get.

I kissed her, hard and deep, and her mouth welcomed my tongue. Her hands rose up my chest, and I groaned at her willing touch. Then they went lower and rubbed the front of my jeans. I throbbed.

I reached out for her and tugged down the last bit of fabric concealing her body. As I kneeled to ease them past her full ass and thighs, I stopped to give her a long lick between her legs. I inhaled her scent. She was fucking delicious. She curled her pelvis into me and put her hand on my head to steady herself. I didn't give her more than a lick as I slipped down her panties. She tugged at my hair in longing.

I wanted her to want it.

She kicked her panties aside, and my hands trailed up her body as I stood. My mouth found hers again. Instead of anger, desire fueled the intensity of her kiss. When I unzipped my jeans, she trembled.

I slipped down my jeans and boxers, guided her toward the bed, and laid her on her back. When she tried to lift the blindfold, I pinned her wrists above her head. My kisses wandered down her chest until I could flick her nipples with my tongue. She whimpered, and it made me throb. I gripped and rubbed my painfully hard cock.

I released her wrists from the grasp of my other hand and rubbed my fingers where she dripped. I leaned between her legs and caught her wetness with my tongue. With her taste in my mouth, I kissed her once more.

She bit her lip as I drew away from her. "Please," she whispered. It wasn't the same pleading that came with her protests. No, it was begging. She was begging me for it.

I dropped between her legs and obliged her, licking in long strokes along her swollen clit. Her chest rose from the mattress, and one of her hands reached for the sheets as the other grabbed the flesh of her chest. A moan left her lips as she gripped the sheet. I put my fingers inside her, feeling her tight, willing pussy—dripping wet and wanting more. I filled her with my fingers, pushing them in and out of her while my tongue flicked at her clit. She trembled and her thighs tightened around me so hard that I had to pull away from her clit to grab her inner thighs, smearing her wetness on one of them as I spread her open. If I could have talked, I would have told her to keep her thighs spread for me, give me full access to her perfect fucking pussy. Instead, I opened her silently before dropping and devouring her once more.

She gripped my hair. "I'm going to come," she whispered.

I wanted to tell her to come for me, but I couldn't. I just pushed my fingers deeper into her and ate her like she was the last thing I'd ever eat. Like a man on death row. I was preparing to leave, but not without a belly full of her.

She came. Hard. An orgasm that lingered in the air through her panting breaths. I climbed up her body and kissed her. She took my face between her hands, rubbing her fingers along the stubble of my beard as if she were reading braille.

I rested my aching cock against her warm, still-twitching pussy. I gripped myself and rubbed the head along her skin, closer to where I wanted to be the most—deep inside her.

I watched her for any signs that she wanted me to stop. Her hands were loose at her sides, releasing the fabric. She bit her lower lip. Her hips moved subtly, rubbing herself against my cock.

I pushed inside her, and a sharp breath left her lips. She felt so goddamn good. Spread open for me, she looked so incredible. I rubbed her thighs, raking my nails down her sensitive skin. She moaned as I thrust as far as I could go inside her, bottoming out just before the hilt of my dick. I was too preoccupied with how her pussy felt around my cock to notice her hands creeping toward her face. I didn't notice until I saw her intense green eyes staring back at me.

At *me*. Not anyone else.

My breath hitched. I expected her to start struggling as I waited for her guilt to suck away her pleasure. Instead, her lips crept into a smile and she pulled me into her for a kiss. Her legs wrapped around me as I buried myself deeper inside her, grinding my pelvis into hers.

"Fuck, little girl," I growled as I pulled away from her mouth. She gazed up at me with a look that made me want to stay. But I couldn't. She knew I couldn't. Her nails dug into my back as I fucked her. "Mouth or pussy?" I asked.

She knew the rules, even if the game was almost over.

"My pussy," she whispered before tucking her face into the crook of my neck.

I knew the release was coming. The moment she looked at me and I knew she wasn't afraid of the boogeyman between her legs, it drew pleasure from my balls. I'd happily fill her pussy. I came, growling as my hips pulsed against hers and my slow thrusts savored our final moments, trying to commit how it felt to my memory.

I lay beside her, come still dripping from us both, and took her into my arms. Her head lay on my chest, her breasts sweaty and sticky against me. My spent cock rested against my thigh, and I blew out a breath.

"I'm going to miss you, little girl," I whispered. "And your smart-ass mouth." I smirked. I tried to make a joke out of it. I tried to hide my true feelings. I didn't want to leave. But I had to. I kept reminding myself I had no choice.

I kissed her forehead and realized just how much she looked like she wanted to say something to me. Her eyes were pleading.

"Are you sure you have to go?" she finally asked as her breaths evened out.

I put a hand over her flushed cheek. "You know I do. I'd stay if I could." There was so much more I wanted to experience with her. Hell, even this cuddling thing, where she fit so perfectly against me.

"I don't think I can go back to my normal life," she whispered. She had to. Her normal life was good for her. "After the car accident, I was never the same. I put everything into work and school. I gave myself no time to get lost in my thoughts." She sighed. "You've forced me to confront feelings I've repressed for so long. You've silenced my thoughts. I could only focus on you between my legs. You've made me feel alive again, Cole. And I hate it, but it's true."

I swallowed. A trapped breath stalled the movement of my chest. She revived me just as much, but there was nothing I could do about it. We needed to stay alive . . . apart.

"I know, little girl. I wish I knew you before I did what I did." I hugged her tighter against my chest.

She was the *one* thing I didn't regret about all the horrible things I'd done. In a world of darkness, she was fucking light.

CHAPTER 14

I fell asleep with her, which I had tried my damndest not to do. Waking up beside her, like we were some normal couple, was heavenly.

But this wasn't heaven. It was purgatory, and I was on my way to hell.

"Please," she whispered as I brushed her hair back from her face.

I drew her pistol from behind my back and smiled at her as I put the safety on and placed it in her hand.

"You know I can't stay, little girl," I said, and it was the most painful truth I'd ever faced. Her eyes glossed and when she rolled them up to me, a tear fell from each one.

Fuck, her pain hurt me.

I pulled her into my chest and hugged her. She had no idea just how much she changed my life. I'd never get past what I'd done before her, but I had to focus on what was ahead of me instead of behind. I wished it could be with her. I would have given almost anything for the situation to be different, that we'd met in some other life or some other time besides my lowest point when my world imploded. I couldn't stay and have her clean up the aftermath any longer.

She was confused. I made her feel things she hadn't in a long time. But I was the wrong person to make her feel so alive. She'd find someone that didn't have such a bloody past. Someone who didn't need to force her to make her want to sleep with them, even if she'd started to love it. It was unhealthy for her to enjoy that so much. To enjoy *me* that much.

I fell in love with her.

Her eyes leapt up to mine, and they widened and deepened. She looked so goddamn sad. "I'm falling for you, Cole. I know I shouldn't, but I can't stand the thought of you leaving," she said with choked words. "I want you to stay with me. We'll make it work somehow. Or hey, maybe just until you get a new job." There was a rise in her voice, a bit of desperation in her words.

I loved her, but I couldn't love her.

I kissed the top of her head. "You be good, little girl. And lock your back door."

Goodbyes like that hurt. They killed. Reminding myself it was all for her was the only way I could close that door behind me over the sounds of her soft cries.

THE FLUORESCENT LIGHTS above the shitty motel bed hummed. I couldn't fucking sleep. Even when I wrapped the pillow around my head, I couldn't drown out that hum.

Leaving Vanessa was the hardest thing I'd ever done. Much harder than what got me on drugs. Her heart had broken, and the way she begged me to stay broke mine. She said she was falling for me, and I left without saying any of it back, which was the ultimate fuck you. If I told her I loved her, it would have been impossible for me to leave. And I needed to go.

I abandoned sleep and went out on the shitty "patio," which was just the broken concrete in front of the peeling white motel door with two rusty chairs on either side. The metal scraped along the concrete as I sat down, and it was like I blew the drug-dealer whistle. Hidden beneath a black jacket and hat, a man smoking a cigarette walked past me. He stopped, turned toward me, and gestured with his chin. My stomach twisted. The temptation was there, gnawing at my insides.

I didn't need to do meth. I could do something else. Just a little taste of something to take the edge off. I reached down to pull out my wallet, but realized I left it inside.

I looked back at the man and shook my head. It was the universe telling me to stay the fuck away from drugs. Most of all, Vanessa would be disappointed in me. But what did that matter, anyway? I'd never see her again. I had to make sure of that.

I went back inside and collapsed on my bed. The hard mattress squealed beneath me. I looked at the Steri-Strips—well, what hadn't fallen off already—on the palm of my hand, and I ached for her. It was just a stupid fucking reminder of all the things I'd lost and then found. And then lost again.

I rolled onto my back and looked up at the leaky ceiling. Brown watermarks snaked along a large crack down the middle. It reminded me of holding her cut and taking care of her. I had a purpose again, having been without one for quite some time.

My mind replayed it all. The moment I saw her. The things I thought that somehow became reality. How she drew me deeper inside her as I fucked her. What the fuck even happened? And why did I let it slip from my hands?

We couldn't be anything.

Could we?

No, we couldn't.

I CRUMPLED the bus ticket in my pocket, holding it in a tight ball in my sweating fist. What was I doing? Being fucking stupid, which was not entirely a new thing for me. My legs were tired without the mania of meth. Though I could still hear the rumble of buses in the distance, I felt as if I'd walked miles.

The familiar light came into view. The home looked just as attractive when I was sober as it did when I was high and seeking sanctuary. It still felt like safety.

I made my way across the large yard, the grass still manicured and well taken care of. I could only stay away for a few days. I think I made it three. Three horrible fucking days where Vanessa played in my head on repeat until I thought I would go crazy if I didn't see her.

So I went to see her.

I tried the handle on the front door, but it was locked. Good girl. I went to the back door. The screen was still ripped, and part of it loosely swayed in the cool night air. I reached for the handle, and it opened. "Goddamn it, little girl," I whispered. I might have been a monster, but there were bigger and badder demons than me out there who would tear her to shreds. Break her.

I stepped inside, carefully taking my shoes off and putting them out of sight.

I waited.

It felt familiar.

It felt like fucking forever.

I heard the key in the front door, and I got behind it, just like I had before. She walked inside, stripping off her coat. When she turned away, I pounced on her. She screamed before my hand covered her mouth, silencing her. She whimpered and flailed out of instinct, and her eyes glistened with panic. Until she saw me. Until she felt the familiarity of my grasp. Until she heard my voice.

"Don't stop fighting me, little girl."

Epilogue

Two things in this world gave me a mind-bending high. One was meth, obviously. The other was Vanessa.

Did we play rough? Yeah. Did she recoil from my touch? Actually, yeah, sometimes. Did I leave her a trembling mess from orgasms after we played? Always. Every damn time. I wouldn't finish until she had a mind-bending high of her own.

I loved her, and I made sure she knew it.

Vanessa awoke a beast in me. One that still couldn't look at her without wanting to rip her clothes off. One that still snuck up on her to catch her off guard, to feel that moment of fear before I fucked her. I wasn't the only one who had a beast, though.

Mine roared and hers purred.

After she finished school, I didn't know what was next for us or what would become of us. I didn't know if she'd ever get sick of my addiction to her. I only knew that she was the single most important thing in my life. My savior. And I'd do *anything* to keep her happy.

I'd never have guessed that an act done during the lowest moment of my life would take me to heaven instead of hell and make an angel fall in love with a demon. Or awaken a beast that played so well with hers.

Connect with Lauren

Check out LaurenBiel.com to sign up for the newsletter and get VIP (free and first) access to Lauren's spicy novellas and other bonus content!

Join the group on Facebook to connect with other fans and to discuss the books with the author. Visit http://www.facebook.com/groups/laurenbieltraumances for more!

Lauren is now on Patreon! Get access to even more content and sneak peeks at upcoming novels. Check it out at www.patreon.com/LaurenBielAuthor to learn more!

ACKNOWLEDGMENTS

Thank you to my husband for still loving me through this journey.

Special thanks to my editor for going on another dark journey she probably didn't want to be on and still helping me be the best I can be.

Also by Lauren Biel

Novels

Shoot Down the Stars

Colliding Stars

The Room to the West

Never Let Go

AfterWife

Novellas

Toxic Love

Toxic Desires

Men of Mayhem

Men of Vengeance

ABOUT THE AUTHOR

Lauren Biel is an author with several titles in the works. When she's not working, she's writing. When she's not writing, she's spending time with her husband, her friends, or her pets. You might also find her on a horseback trail ride or sitting beside a waterfall in Upstate New York. When reading her work, expect the unexpected.

To be the first to know about her upcoming titles, please visit www.LaurenBiel.com.